As an angel, Mordecai has the ability to read the thoughts of others. Sitting in a coffee shop, eyeing the human he's there to help—Charles—Mordecai listens to the man's internal troubles so he can discern the best way to assist him. Mordecai hears Charles wondering why he's agreed to meet his workout buddy, Jeffrey, for coffee . . . knowing Jeffrey intends it as a date. According to Charles's thoughts, the human has never bothered acting on his occasional flash of appreciation for the opposite sex, and he doesn't see the point in doing so now.

Mordecai assumes that his task is to help Charles come to grips with his desire for the occasional male. In the past, he's spent time talking with his assigned human, walking them through a bit of soul-searching. Mordecai doesn't think anything is special about the assignment. He's done it plenty of times before.

Everything changes when Mordecai gets his first look at Jeffrey and meets the man's gaze. The human, Jeffrey—Charles's date—is his *stella guida*, his guiding star—the one human he can share a soul with. How can Mordecai help Charles come to grips with dating Jeffrey, when every instinct screams at him to take him for his own?

An Angelic Dilemma

ISBN: 978-1-4874-3795-4
Cover art by Angela Waters

Published by eXtasy Books Inc

Look for us online at:
www.eXtasybooks.com

An Angelic Dilemma
A Loving Nip: Book Thirty

By

Charlie Richards

Dedication

Just do it.
~Nike tag line

Chapter One

Sitting on the park bench, Mordecai peered at the clock tower attached to the town's city hall. He read the time, wondering how much longer it would be before the mark of his current mission would be finished at the gym down the street—a human named Charles Rickter. He'd casted a mental web spell earlier that morning, allowing him to track the man's location. Mordecai intended to follow him and find a suitable place to bump into the human and spark up a friendship.

As an angel, Mordecai enjoyed sitting and relaxing, so he didn't mind waiting. People watching, he'd heard it called. He found humans fascinating, with their diverse sizes, shapes, colors, and sexes, spawning so many ideas and beliefs.

Of course, those same myriad of ideas and beliefs were also what created the need for Mordecai's kind. Angels lived on another plane of existence and were tasked with keeping emotional and spiritual peace between humans. Considering the fighting and quarrels humans and paranormals alike seemed to constantly participate in, Mordecai didn't think they were doing a very good job.

Fortunately, Mordecai wasn't alone in that conclusion. He and his brethren had decided to step up their presence in the human realm as much as possible between missions given to them by their creator. Their creator saw the souls of every being in the realm, and he assigned an angel to help those who were going through a personal crisis.

That was why Mordecai sat waiting for Charles. He would need to be closer to the human to listen to his thoughts, allowing him to learn what troubled the man. Then he could devise a way to assist.

As Mordecai sat waiting, he cast out his senses. The mental ability allowed him to listen to the thoughts of those closest to him.

His reasons for that were two-fold.

First, Mordecai would be happy to help calm the thoughts or bolster the spirits of anyone nearby who needed it. Secondly, Mordecai knew there were paranormal hunters out there.

A fellow angel—Zylen—had been captured and held by them, although the general consensus was that Zylen had ended up in the wrong place at the wrong time. The hunters seemed to have mistaken him for another paranormal and had then been uncertain about what to do with him. Fortunately, before the humans had come to a decision about Zylen, he'd been rescued by the Four Horsemen of the Apocalypse.

When the Four Horsemen had sent several demons to the creator's realm, it had caused quite a stir.

The harried thoughts of a woman shuffling down the sidewalk nearby caught Mordecai's attention.

I just don't know how to get through to him. Kyle just won't listen. He used to be such a good boy.

Mordecai turned his attention to the young teenager following a few paces behind the woman. He immediately noted the familial link joining them, seen only by angels and demons, and he knew they were mother and son. Mordecai also took in his hunched shoulders and sulking, mutinous expression. His thoughts were just as telling.

I don't see what the big deal is. It's not like the store can't afford to lose a few bucks just because I stole a couple of candy bars. Me and my buddies wanted them.

With a shake of his head, Mordecai rose from the bench. He had his glamour firmly in place, hiding his angelic aura as well as his wings. Keeping his wings tucked close to his back, Mordecai moved swiftly, putting himself in a position where he would pass them on the sidewalk.

The mother—Constance, his angelic abilities provided—peered at him discreetly from beneath her lashes. Her cheeks pinked just a little, and she quickly shifted her gaze forward. He caught the scent of arousal, letting him know she found him appealing.

Mordecai was always flattered when that happened, regardless of how often it occurred. As an angel, he knew he was built big and broad. He had the body of a warrior with solid muscles and a trim waist. Many humans, women and men alike, seemed to find it appealing.

Of course, Mordecai would never act on it. In truth, he couldn't. An angel didn't experience any sexual impulses. At least, not until they met their *stella guida*—their guiding star—the one person they could bond with and build a life with outside of their duties to their creator.

Concentrating on the matter at hand, Mordecai opened his mind as he brushed his fingertips over the back of the young man's hand while passing him—Kyle. In that fleeting contact, he learned that Kyle had made a couple of new friends at school. They were a bad influence on him, filling his head with entitle-ist and selfish ideas.

Kyle was beginning to think the world owed him, and he should have whatever he wanted without working for it. It didn't matter that his single mother worked two jobs to keep a roof over their heads and food on the table. His schoolwork had begun to slip because Kyle wanted to play video games with friends instead of putting in the time and energy to get decent grades, which would lead to him having opportunities to better himself.

In that same second or two, Mordecai implanted a few thoughts of his own. He boosted the pride Kyle would feel at completing a task, at seeing a job well done. Mordecai added a wealth of empathy for his mother and a surge of respect for how hard she worked to provide for him. He even added in a bit of apathy so he wouldn't care what his new friends might think of his sudden desire to work hard and help his mother. Mordecai added the knowledge that life wasn't all about fun, as it came with responsibilities.

Frowning, Kyle stepped to the left, away from Mordecai's touch. He heard the young man's thoughts. *Geez, stay in your lane, jerk.* That was fine. Mordecai had done what he could.

Hmmm . . . maybe I can do one more thing.

With a quick mental chant, Mordecai cast a silent spell.

Constance tripped over nothing, stumbling a step. She flailed a bit, trying to catch her balance.

Mordecai pivoted and caught her arm, lending her support.

"Oh, goodness," Constance murmured, her cheeks darkening with embarrassment. "Thank you, sir."

"You're welcome, miss," Mordecai replied. With his free hand, he squeezed her hand lightly. "Happy to help."

As Mordecai spoke, he pushed into her mind. He shared the names and poor influence of Kyle's new school chums. Mordecai gave her the fortitude to hold the course and help her son straighten himself out.

Mordecai dipped his chin in a silent goodbye as he offered her a small smile. Then he released her and headed on his way. Spotting Charles exiting the gym, Mordecai matched his stride and followed him.

To Mordecai's relief, Charles didn't head to a vehicle. Instead, he crossed the street at the corner and opened the door to a coffee café. Mordecai quickly entered behind him and spotted him already at the counter.

As Mordecai moved into the line behind Charles, he

heard him order a protein drink. He mentally cringed at the sound of it, and when it came to his own turn, he asked for a berry smoothie. Mordecai gave the barista his name before following Charles toward the pick-up area as he listened to the human's thoughts.

What the hell am I doing here? Charles didn't sound particularly happy. *I shouldn't have agreed to meet Jeffrey. If I'd known he would think of this as a date, I would have turned him down.* After giving a mental groan, Charles continued his mental rant. *How did I let him catch me looking at his ass? Except, those running shorts he wears make it look so damn sexy. How could I* not *notice?*

Charles took his drink from the barista before Mordecai could think up a way to introduce himself.

Leaning an arm against the counter, Mordecai discreetly watched Charles head to a table off to the left.

Maybe I can set Jeffrey straight as soon as he arrives. We don't have to have a drink together. Charles eyed the door as he took a sip of his beverage. *Or I'll let him know I'm flattered, but I don't swing his way.* Scowling at his drink, Charles twisted his lips into a pensive expression. *I'll just explain that I enjoy the male form, but I don't wanna cross that line. God, I hope he understands. I don't wanna be labeled bisexual. Just because I find men nice to look at on occasion doesn't mean I want to do anything with them.*

As Mordecai had continued listening to Charles's tense musings, he'd received his drink and sat down at a nearby table. He realized the human found himself attracted to another man, but he obviously wasn't ready to cross that line. Mordecai had dealt with plenty of men just like Charles over the last several decades.

While it was becoming more accepted to be labeled gay or bisexual—and humans had even come up with a myriad of other labels to try to fit people into nice little boxes—some people were still finding it tough to accept some of their urges. Being gay, straight, bi, or whatever didn't matter. Humans and paranormals alike were made in the creator's image, and it was them who'd come up with the prejudices.

Charles was leaning toward denying his urges, and Mordecai knew it was his job to make certain that if the human did that, it wasn't going to damage his psyche in any way.

Just as Mordecai decided to ask Charles about his drink—he knew he was a built, fit guy, and could pass it off as a health-related question—the door to the café opened, and the bell jingled. He saw Charles's shoulders stiffen. Following the human's line of sight, Mordecai watched as a tall blond man swept his gaze over the café.

When the man's gaze landed on Mordecai, for an instant, it remained there. The man's green eyes widened, and his nostrils flared. He even froze just within the entrance.

Mordecai felt that look right down to his toes. His breath caught in his chest, and it felt as if the world tilted on its axis. He felt his blood begin to heat, warming him from the inside out.

For the first time in Mordecai's life, he felt his dick begin to swell, and a tingle warmed his groin. His fingers twitched around his cup, and he longed to thread them through the human's damp-looking hair. The thick locks were just long enough to fall across his forehead, and Mordecai wanted to push them from the man's gorgeous face.

I could peer into his beautiful green eyes as I run my fingers along his jaw. Would I feel a fine hint of scruff there? What would that feel like across my palm . . . or chest . . . or—

"Hey, Jeffrey," Charles greeted, and the man yanked his attention from Mordecai and turned to the other human.

Just that fast, Mordecai realized two very important things. The human was Jeffrey, the man who'd asked Charles on a date. And second, Jeffrey was his *stella guida*—his guiding star.

Oh, dear creator. Mordecai couldn't help the mental anguish coursing through him as he watched Jeffrey greet Charles with a smile and chin lift. *How can I objectively help Charles through this decision?*

"Let me get a drink, and I'll be right there," Jeffrey told Charles. A wry smile curved his full lips as he added, "From your expression, I know what's coming, and I think you'll be surprised at my response."

"Uh, okay," Charles replied, sounding confused.

When Jeffrey reached the counter and began talking to the woman behind it, Mordecai rose. He quickly made his way out of the café. Unable to help himself, he paused in the doorway and glanced over his shoulder.

Mordecai sucked in a harsh breath as he spotted Jeffrey staring after him, and a jolt of longing slammed into him . . . hard.

Clenching his jaw, Mordecai turned and headed away from both men—his mark and his *stella guida.*

One thought circled his brain.

How can I help Charles make a fair decision when I want Jeffrey all to myself?

CHAPTER TWO

Unable to help himself, Jeffrey Aalders watched the stunningly gorgeous man exit the coffee café. He felt sweat bead at his temples, and his belly even bumped with butterflies. His dick thickened to half-mast, and it took every last shred of self-control Jeffrey had to keep from springing a hard-as-nails boner.

Never had Jeffrey ever felt a jolt of lust so strong. From the answering heat in the large man's unique, aqua-colored eyes, he knew the man was just as attracted. Too bad the guy couldn't seem to get out of the place fast enough.

For just an instant, when the stranger had paused in the doorway and looked back at him, Jeffrey had held out a smidgen of hope.

Just another classic closet case. Damn.

Heading to the counter to pick up his drink, Jeffrey did his best to shove his disappointment way down deep. He hadn't felt a connection like that in . . . well, ever, if he were being honest. Jeffrey would have loved to have explored what they could mean to each other.

Or we could have just had one hell of a one-night stand.

While Jeffrey would love to find a nice guy to call his own, he knew that not everyone was wired for monogamy. His brother, Jarvis, was in a ménage with a man and a woman. Jeffrey never presumed to judge, and he'd enjoyed a ménage a few times, but over the years, he'd learned he preferred the one-on-one experience.

Evidently, the sexy-as-sin guy who'd just fled wasn't

ready even for that.

Too bad.

Turning his attention to Charles—his would-be date—Jeffrey did his best to put the hottie out of his mind. It was hard, though. The way the handsome man's thick, dark-brown hair had been pulled from his face in a half ponytail, like the warriors of old, had accentuated his aristocratic features.

Shit. Get your head out of your ass, dipshit.

Jeffrey forced a slight smile as he settled with his strawberry-flavored protein shake in the chair opposite Charles. "So, it only took me the couple of minutes while taking my shower in the changing room to realize I'd shocked the shit out of you, and you were just being polite." With a smirk, Jeffrey took in Charles's surprised expression. He shrugged, allowing his smile to widen. Lowering his voice, he murmured, "Sure, I saw you checking out my ass, but I'm gay as the day is long, and I've checked out women's asses." With a shrug, Jeffrey leaned closer, resting his elbows on the table. "You're not that into me. I get that."

Charles blew out a breath. His expression betrayed his relief as clear as day. With a wry smile, he nodded once.

"Damn, I was worried," Charles admitted. Lifting one hand, he rubbed the back of his neck. Charles kept his voice low as he told him, "I thought maybe you'd push because . . . I don't know. You saw me and took the time to ask. You knew I found at least something about you attractive, so—"

When Charles's brows furrowed and he snapped his mouth shut, Jeffrey did his best to squash his annoyance. Not every gay man would push a straight guy—even one who maybe wasn't so straight—to date just because they were caught looking. Jeffrey had to remember that he didn't really know Charles all that well. They worked out together at the gym a couple of times a week when their leg and arm days coincided.

Jeffrey concentrated on cardio and muscle toning, strengthening his muscles and lung capacity for running marathons. Charles, on the other hand, easily pushed more weights. He focused on muscle building, especially his torso, which sported wonderfully defined pectorals and a ripped six-pack.

Which is probably why I jumped at the possibility of getting a chance to explore him. A little too eagerly, it would seem.

On the other hand, now I have a brand new sexy fantasy man to occupy my spank bank fantasies.

"It's fine, Charles," Jeffrey assured, lifting the straw of his smoothie to his lips. He relaxed back in his seat after taking a drink. "Really." Knowing a subject change was in order, Jeffrey decided to go with, "Even though this didn't happen quite like I'd thought, it's nice to chat with you outside the gym." Jeffrey had toyed with the idea of expanding their pseudo-friendship for a while. "I know you work as an attorney and are madly addicted to those horrible shakes." Smirking, he pointed at the green concoction in Charles's cup. "Other than work out your very nice muscles, what do you do for fun?"

"Hey. I'll have you know that these awesome drinks fuel these very fine muscles." Even as Charles took on a mock-annoyed tone, he smirked and lifted his arm, flexing his bicep, showing off the exquisite bulge. "And you obviously enjoy looking at them very much."

Jeffrey lifted his hands, palms out. "Guilty as charged."

To Jeffrey's surprise, Charles narrowed his eyes and smirked. "Although, not as much as you enjoyed checking out that big, dark-haired guy that left right after you came in."

Feeling his cheeks take on just a little warmth, Jeffrey scoffed depreciatively. "Uh, yeah. Caught that, huh?"

Charles nodded once, a true smile curving his lips. "I

did." With a scoff, he admitted, "Made me feel a little better, to be honest."

"Why?" Jeffrey asked curiously before sipping his drink.

Shrugging, Charles told him, "Between your words and the way you were eye-fucking that guy, figured you weren't really that into me." He smirked, adding, "Your words confirmed it, and it meant I didn't have to figure out some nice way to let you down easy."

Barking a laugh, Jeffrey nodded. "Got it." With a wistful sigh, he allowed his gaze to stray to the door. "He sure was hot."

Charles nodded and responded, "That he was."

Jeffrey's brows shot up.

Arching one brow, Charles reminded, "We already established that we both know how to appreciate a fine specimen, regardless of the sex, even if we have no interest in sleeping with said specimen."

Nodding once more, Jeffrey replied, "Fair enough."

"He gave you an appreciative look, if I'm not mistaken," Charles pointed out. "Think he's a regular here?"

Jeffrey shrugged. "Even if he is, he sure hot-footed it out of here fast." He grimaced, muttering, "Probably in the closet."

"You don't know that," Charles countered. "Maybe he just had somewhere to be." Tapping the table with his forefinger, he offered, "Let's meet here after working out on Wednesday, and we'll see if he turns up again."

Surprised at Charles's show of support, Jeffrey nodded even as he struggled with something to say. "You didn't happen to catch his name after you ordered, did you?"

Grimacing, Charles shook his head. "Naw. Sorry, man." A slight hint of pink crept up the broader man's neck. "Was too, uh . . ."

"Having a mental freak-out?" Jeffrey couldn't help but

tease. When Charles winced, he offered, "Sorry about that, by the way. Never meant to make you uncomfortable."

Charles rolled his large shoulders negligently. "No biggie." Tapping his chest, he grinned widely and waggled his eyebrows. "I'm a hot guy. How could you *not* notice?"

Jeffrey chuckled as he shook his head, appreciating the levity. Taking another drink, he couldn't help but think of the big stranger. The way his aqua eyes had appeared to deepen to the greenish end of the spectrum had caused his breath to catch. The man was, in a word, stunning.

"You're thinking about him," Charles cut into his thoughts. With a soft scoff, he added, "Sorry I didn't catch his name for you."

"Probably for the best," Jeffrey countered, once more reminding himself that the handsome man had dashed out the door. "Do you—"

Before Jeffrey could finish his question, Reagan Suthers settled on a chair at their table, interrupting. "His name's Mordecai. I was listening when he told the barista his name," he stated, his expression imperious. "And don't even bother going after that angel. He's mine." Reagan's lips curved into a lascivious smile as he glanced toward the table where the stranger—Mordecai—had been seated. "I can't wait to have someone like that on my arm. The things I'll be able to accomplish." Just as quickly, Reagan rose to his feet. He pinned Jeffrey with a withering look. "So don't even bother trying. Mordecai is mine."

Then Reagan sauntered out of the coffee café, taking his air of superiority with him.

"I can't count the number of times I've wanted to deck that guy," Charles rumbled, crossing his arms over his chest. He shook his head as he flexed his muscles, obviously irritated. "He's such a pompous ass."

Jeffrey nodded his agreement as he watched Reagan

saunter toward a high-end, newer-model *BMW*. Once he was out of sight, he refocused on Charles.

"Reagan's what? Three, four years younger than us?" Jeffrey shook his head as he added, "I'm thirty-two, by the way. Guess I was making an assumption."

Charles nodded, his annoyed expression easing. "Thirty-three, but yeah. That'd be my guess."

"How the hell is he a partner in the firm he's working at already?"

Jeffrey vaguely recalled Reagan from high school a decade and a half before. He'd been a senior when the other man had been a freshman. They hadn't run in the same circles—Jeffrey playing sports and Reagan focusing on academics—but he'd still noticed the way the guy tried to bully others.

Then Jeffrey had graduated. He'd skipped college and immediately gone to work with a landscaping company. He loved working outdoors and with his hands. It'd been the perfect fit. After over a decade with them, Jeffrey was a project manager, but he still helped with the physical aspects of a job often.

Jeffrey hadn't given Reagan any thought until he'd joined their gym. He still had no idea why. Surely the high-end apartment building he loved to brag about had its own facilities.

"I heard Reagan's sleeping with one of the senior partners," Charles responded softly. As an attorney himself, although not at the same firm, he would probably know. He leaned forward, lowering his voice further. "A married guy, and they share his wife."

Wincing, Jeffrey cocked his head. "My brother's in a ménage relationship," he admitted, rubbing the back of his neck. "So that doesn't bother me, but sleeping with them to get ahead? That's wrong, man."

Charles shrugged. "Just what I heard."

Thinking of Reagan's high-handed, entitle-ist attitude, Jeffrey shrugged. "Guess I could see it, though." Then he squinted at Charles. "Think he was telling the truth? That the hot guy's name is Mordecai?"

Nodding, Charles told him, "With the way Reagan told us, as if to lord it over us, yeah. The guy's name is Mordecai."

Jeffrey thought on that for a second, before saying, "I almost want to track Mordecai down just to warn him about Reagan."

"I know, right?" Charles agreed. After a second, he added, "Well, if we can believe Reagan about Mordecai's name, then we can believe him about the other thing."

"Other thing?" Jeffrey wasn't following.

Charles smirked. "That Mordecai is out enough for Reagan to know it."

Jeffrey chuckled softly, his blood heating in his veins as he thought about that. "Yeah," he whispered.

Mordecai is out. Maybe he did just need to get somewhere.

Hope I see him again so I have the chance to find out.

Chapter Three

Sweeping his gaze over the grasses and trees that made up one of the many pastures at Rolling Meadows Ranch and Resort, Mordecai searched for his fellow angel. He felt Malakai's signature and knew he had to be close. A second later, he spotted the man riding a large black horse, trotting along the fence line.

Beside Malakai rode another man—the angel's vampire *stella guida,* Murdoch.

Mordecai immediately lowered the shield that had kept him hidden from prying eyes. While he didn't think he would have any problems with the vampires, shifters, and humans that lived and worked at the ranch, he didn't want to answer any questions. At least, not from them. Mordecai needed the advice of another angel, and he felt blessed that Malakai was only a few towns over from where his mark and *stella guida* were living.

Mordecai spread his wings and flew toward Malakai, instantly drawing the other angel's attention. Both men stopped and dismounted. While Murdoch secured their mounts to a tree, Malakai strode slowly in his direction.

Landing before the fellow angel, Mordecai held out his right hand. Malakai gripped his wrist, and Mordecai did the same. They pulled each other in for a brief, one-armed hug before stepping back and releasing each other.

"Mordecai," Malakai greeted with a warm smile. "It's good to see you, brother."

Mordecai knew that Malakai used the term brother loosely. Technically, because angels weren't born but were made by the creator, they were all brothers. Each and every one of them shared what humans would call similar DNA.

"You as well, brother," Mordecai replied. Although, from the way Malakai arched one brow, he figured his return smile looked more like a grimace. With a sigh, Mordecai admitted softly, "I've failed the creator."

Malakai's second brow lifted to join the first. "I must admit, I have a difficult time believing that," he commented. Resting a hand on Mordecai's shoulder, he squeezed lightly. "Tell me about it."

Mordecai opened his mouth, then paused as he spotted Murdoch approaching. "I'm interrupting your time with your *stella guida,*" he murmured, rubbing at his chest, the ache within him reminding him where he wished he could be—with his own guiding star. "Perhaps I should—"

"Nonsense," Murdoch cut in, having obviously overheard. The vampire offered his hand. "I'm Murdoch, although you probably already know that."

Taking Murdoch's hand, Mordecai returned the shake. "I did. I'm Mordecai. My apologies for interrupting."

Murdoch shook his head as he slipped his arm around Malakai's waist. "Not at all. We're just riding fence together." With a roguish grin, Murdoch waggled his brows at Malakai. "I never tire of riding the perimeter with my beloved."

Malakai rumbled softly, chuckling quietly. His eyes narrowed, heat filling their aqua depths. "That's because you love spending the night with me out beneath the stars."

His expression softening, Murdoch replied, "I love spending the night with you anywhere, Malakai."

"The feeling is mutual, my vampire," Malakai rumbled huskily. A second later, he dipped his head and sealed his mouth over Murdoch's, taking him in a deep kiss.

Having never seen an angel engage in anything carnal,

Mordecai found his lips parting in surprise. He snapped his mouth closed just as quickly. Suddenly, Mordecai wondered what Jeffrey would taste like.

Would my stella guida allow me to do that to him? Even in front of others?

That brought Mordecai right back to his predicament.

How do I accomplish my mission? How do I help my mark when it could include accepting his feelings for another man . . . who just happens to be Jeffrey?

Malakai snapped his head up, breaking the kiss. His eyes widened as he yanked his focus to Mordecai. Even his lips parted in obvious surprise.

Mordecai winced. "I projected that, didn't I?"

Nodding even as he rubbed his hand up and down Murdoch's back, Malakai murmured, "Yes. You were worked up enough to allow your thoughts to slip through your mental shields."

Due to an angel's natural ability to pick up the thoughts of those around them, when they were backed by enough emotion, each angel knew how to erect a mental shield. That way, they weren't constantly hearing each other while on their natural plane.

"Sorry about that," Mordecai muttered before letting out a sigh. "I—" He paused, then admitted, "I met my *stella guida*."

"Congrats, man." Murdoch grinned as he reached over and slapped Mordecai on the upper arm. "So what the fuck are you doing here?"

Mordecai winced upon hearing the vampire's coarse language.

Or maybe it's because I fear admitting my folly.

Malakai smirked as he lifted one shoulder in a half-shrug. "Living in the human realm, you grow more tolerant of peoples' word choices," he stated with a shake of his head.

Murdoch rolled his eyes. "Hey. You were thinkin' it," he

teased with a smirk. "I'm just sayin' it."

Chuckling softly, Malakai nodded. "I was indeed thinking something similar," he admitted. Reaching out, he gripped Mordecai's shoulder and squeezed lightly. "What are you doing here?" Then Malakai frowned, obviously having recalled Mordecai's earlier claim. "How can you believe that finding your *stella guida* means you've failed our creator?"

Mordecai admitted, "I was following my mark, Charles, and learned that he'd been asked on a coffee date by Jeffrey."

"Struggling with sexuality, huh?" Murdoch cut in astutely.

Nodding, Mordecai replied, "I believe so. Yes."

Malakai's eyes widened once more. "You mentioned Jeffrey in your thoughts. He's your *stella guida*?"

Sadness and frustration rolled through Mordecai in waves as he nodded.

"Oh, shit," Murdoch muttered, shaking his head. "The human you're supposed to help was on a date with your *stella guida*?" As Mordecai nodded, the vampire muttered, "Damn. That's rough."

Mordecai mentally agreed.

"What did you do?" Malakai asked softly, his voice full of concern.

Crossing his arms over his chest, Mordecai admitted his folly. "Nothing. I fled." When the pair exchanged a glance, possibly talking telepathically to each other in the way bonded vampires could, Mordecai heaved a sigh. "That's why I failed. I couldn't bear to see my *stella guida* being interested in another. And I left my mark to deal with his uncertainty on his own. I—" Mordecai paused, his voice breaking as pain lashed through him in a way he'd never before experienced. "I left them both to their uncertain fates."

Malakai gripped Mordecai's upper arms in a firm hold.

His gaze was piercing as he stared him in the eyes. "You only fail the creator when you walk away from your mission and don't try." Mordecai was about to point out that that was exactly what he'd done when Malakai stated, "And you are not doing that. Instead, you came for help. For guidance."

Mordecai opened his mouth, then shut it again. Peering into Malakai's serene aqua eyes, the color a little lighter than his own, he realized the other angel was right. Mordecai had sought out Malakai because he was already bonded, and he needed a sounding board.

"So, what do I do?" Mordecai whispered, still confused about how to resolve his dilemma.

"You fight for your *stella guida* while helping your . . . mark, did you call it?" Murdoch stated bluntly, his dark eyes flashing to red, betraying his vampire nature.

"Yes," Mordecai confirmed, staring at the vampire. "The mark of my mission is Charles. I'm supposed to help him."

Malakai squeezed his arms once before releasing him. "That doesn't mean you need to help him by allowing him to become something more to your *stella guida* than friendship."

"Jeffrey was the one who asked out Charles," Mordecai pointed out. Touching his temple, he explained, "I heard Charles's ramblings. He didn't realize it was supposed to be a date when he accepted the invitation to meet Jeffrey at the coffee café."

Cocking his head, Malakai reminded, "In order for you to recognize your *stella guida*, your gazes had to meet."

When the other angel arched one brow in silent question, Mordecai nodded once.

"So, how did Jeffrey react?" Malakai stared intently at him. "Did he glance away? Stare back? Move toward you?"

Mordecai allowed himself to remember that perfect,

spine-tingling moment . . . those few precious seconds when he'd held Jeffrey's attention. His green eyes had held him captivated. He recalled his desire to slide his fingers through the man's damp blond hair, telling him he'd taken a shower after working out with Charles.

Jeffrey's lips had parted, his nostrils had flared, and he'd stared back at Mordecai with open appreciation filling his gorgeous eyes.

Just recalling those precious seconds had an unexpected reaction to his body. Mordecai felt his skin heat, and his gut clenched. He felt goose bumps break out on his arms as blood flowed south, causing his prick to thicken.

"Yeah," Mordecai whispered, nodding slowly. "I understand what you're getting at. He was . . . affected by me, too."

Just as I was affected by him.

"Well, then." Malakai smiled at him. "That means Jeffrey will probably no longer have much of an interest in Charles."

"You think?" Hope filled Mordecai even as he fought his desire to adjust himself. "Jeffrey would pass up dating Charles, even if the man would consider acknowledging his bisexuality, in order to be with me?"

Murdoch groaned as he rolled his eyes. "Damn, you guys really make this more complicated than it needs to be," he stated with a shake of his head. "You're an angel. Jeffrey's your *stella guida*. He's going to want you, even if he doesn't understand why right away." His lips curving into an encouraging smile, the vampire stated, "Really. Just let nature take its course. If Charles is supposed to explore his sexuality, help him do it with someone else." Using a crooked finger to tip his Stetson back a little, Murdoch claimed, "Maybe having Charles see a couple of homosexual couples interacting will help him become more comfortable with his own urges." He wiggled his fingers between himself and Malakai. "We could join you all for a meal. Meet at a nice steakhouse or something?"

Mordecai hummed softly for a few seconds, processing Murdoch's request. The vampire seemed like a genuinely nice guy. He was happy Malakai had ended up with someone so good-hearted.

"What do you mean by having Charles see a *couple* of homosexual couples?" Mordecai asked. "Who's the other couple?"

Malakai chuckled softly. "I think Murdoch means for you and Jeffrey to be the second couple."

"But I don't even know how to find Jeffrey," Malakai countered, frowning as unease filled him. "He's not my mark."

"Mark." Murdoch snickered as he grinned at Mordecai. "Makes you sound like you're an assassin, and you plan to off him."

Mordecai scowled, uncertain how to process that.

Smacking Murdoch's butt, Malakai rumbled, "Behave, my vampire." While Murdoch waggled his brows, not seeming to mind the swat in the least, Malakai turned his attention back to him. "As an angel, you have the ability to track down Charles, so use that."

"What do you mean?" Mordecai was having a hard time concentrating now that he was allowing himself to entertain the possibility of getting close to Jeffrey.

"I mean, you use your connection to Charles to seek him out," Malakai explained, once again wrapping his arm around his vampire. "Then you approach him. Ask him about his friend in the coffee café." With a wide smile, the other angel finished, "That gives you a reason to introduce yourself to Charles, get a second feel for how he views being gay, as well as a chance to meet Jeffrey."

Nodding slowly, Mordecai thought about that idea. It was

a good one. Besides, if that didn't work, he could always haunt the gym until Jeffrey turned up again.

"Thank you," Mordecai stated, relieved upon hearing Malakai's encouragement.

I can figure this out. I can win my stella guida *while still helping Charles.*

My future depends on it.

CHAPTER FOUR

Frowning, Jeffrey stared at the contact information on his screen.

Why would Charles be calling me in the middle of the afternoon? We don't plan to work out together until evening after next.

Could I have made him more uncomfortable than he let on?

They'd ended up chatting for another hour at the coffee café, even getting sandwiches and drink refills. Jeffrey thought he was making a great new friend. They'd talked about when they would meet up to work out together again.

So what's going on?

Knowing there was only one way to find out, Jeffrey answered Charles's call. "Hey, Charles. What's up?"

"You won't believe who just appeared in the diner where I was eating lunch today," Charles stated in lieu of a greeting.

Jeffrey arched one brow as he shifted to his ass on the sod he'd just finished laying. "Uh, no idea." He wasn't a fan of guessing games, and with the mirth that he could hear in Charles's voice, he didn't feel like hazarding a guess.

"Come on, Jeff," Charles urged. "Give me a guess."

With a roll of his eyes, Jeffrey thought quickly. "Uh, Reagan?" He knew the lawyer worked in another building in that area.

"No, thank god," Charles replied.

"Why don't you just tell me who was at the diner?" Jeffrey urged as he scanned the area that he still needed to complete that afternoon. He really didn't have time to be screwing around. "You're obviously excited about it," he added, shifting gears. "Is it some woman you have the hots for?"

"Nope," Charles responded gleefully. "It was Mordecai."

"Mordecai?" Jeffrey would forever deny how breathy he sounded saying the one word.

"Yup." With a laugh, Charles told him, "And he actually knew who I was and asked to sit down with me."

A rush of jealousy surged through Jeffrey like nothing he'd ever felt before. He scowled at the ground before him and clenched his fist. After forcing himself to take a deep breath, Jeffrey managed to push the unexpected reaction way down deep.

"Did you hear me?" Charles asked. "You still there?"

"Yeah. Yeah, I heard you," Jeffrey managed to keep his voice fairly level. "Was just surprised," he told him. Unable to contain his curiosity, he asked, "Uh, what did he want?"

"It was a little odd, actually, now that I think about it," Charles told him slowly, his tone turning hesitant. "We talked about work, about my family, and even if I was dating anyone. The conversation was really easy." Charles paused for a few seconds before admitting, "It almost felt as if he'd been a good buddy for years."

"Wow." Jeffrey's jealousy surged anew, nearly choking him. Somehow, he managed to add inanely, "That's, uh, that's odd."

"I know, right?" Charles cleared his throat. "Then he asked me about you."

Jeffrey sucked in a sharp breath, excitement flooding him. "H-He did?"

Charles had to be grinning when he answered, "That was what I was originally calling to tell you." With a laugh, he added, "Mordecai knew your name and that we work out together. He also wanted to know if you were seeing anyone."

Hearing that, Jeffrey felt his pulse race in his veins. "Shit, really?"

"Yep." Charles sounded damn smug when he stated, "I told him that you weren't and asked him if he'd like me to pass along his cell number." When Jeffrey couldn't get enough saliva into his throat to speak, Charles continued, "He also asked me to pass along the message that he was sorry he didn't stop to meet you yesterday at the coffee café."

"Holy shit," Jeffrey whispered, shocked and ecstatic in equal measure. Doing his best not to sigh or squeal like a high school girl, he cleared his throat instead. "Did he, uh . . . did Mordecai say why he didn't stay?"

"He did not," Charles replied. "Why don't you ask him yourself?"

"Yeah, uh, yeah." Jeffrey rubbed his forehead, trying to get his lust-filled brain to think like a rational adult. "Uh, I don't have a pen handy. I'm laying sod. Can you text me his number?"

"Sure will, buddy," Charles replied, still sounding smug as hell. "Don't overthink it, and give him a call after you get off work," he counseled, surprising Jeffrey. "I know you like this guy." Then Charles growled softly under his breath. "And we sure don't want Reagan to get his greedy little hooks into him. I should have warned him at the diner, but I didn't think of it."

Surprised for a new reason, Jeffrey commented, "You seem sort of invested in keeping Reagan away from Mordecai. Not that I feel any different, but my reasons are wholly selfish." He laughed huskily as all the different things he would like to do to Mordecai's big, gorgeous body filled his mind.

Predictably, Jeffrey's dick began to thicken. He grimaced

as he adjusted himself, finding a more comfortable position. It was a good thing his work jeans were loose-fit.

Just what I need. Working the rest of the afternoon with a boner.

Still, if it meant Jeffrey would get the opportunity to see Mordecai again and actually be able to talk to him, it would be worth it.

Hell, yeah!

"I only talked to Mordecai for a half hour, but he seemed like a decent guy," Charles told him. "I sure wouldn't want Reagan to ruin him."

"No one deserves that," Jeffrey agreed. "So, Mordecai's a nice guy, huh?"

Jeffrey liked hearing that. He wouldn't mind hearing more.

"Well, I've had about as much gossiping like a teenager as I can stand for the day," Charles stated with a laugh. "Plus, I know we both need to get back to work."

Scoffing, Jeffrey admitted, "I was just thinking the same damn thing." Sobering, he rubbed a glove-covered hand over his worn, dirty jeans. "Thanks for helping, man. I appreciate it."

"We all deserve someone good in our life," Charles stated sagely. "See you Wednesday evening."

"See ya." Lowering his phone, Jeffrey saw that Charles had ended the call. "If this guy works out for me, maybe we can find some nice lady for you." Realizing he was getting way ahead of himself, he smirked as he shook his head. "Get your head out of your ass, and get back to work, Jeffrey."

Except, a second later, when his phone chimed and Jeffrey spotted Charles's text with Mordecai's phone number, he couldn't help the way his shaft twitched behind his fly any more than he could stop himself from sporting a goofy grin.

Yep. I'm totally channeling my inner teenage girl.

After showering off the dirt from his workday, Jeffrey grabbed a bottle of unsweetened iced tea and headed to his living room. He carried his cell in his other hand and settled in his reclining chair. After kicking the chair back, instead of turning on the TV, Jeffrey stared at the phone number on his phone's screen.

The tagline for a shoe company floated through his head.

Just do it.

Yep. Good advice.

After swallowing several gulps of his tea to wet his suddenly dry throat, Jeffrey rested the bottle on his knee. Then he hit the dial icon. He lifted the phone to his ear and waited with bated breath.

One ring.

Two.

On the third ring, Jeffrey thought he would have to leave a message. His mind whirled with what he could possibly say.

Hi. This is Jeffrey Aalders. You asked for my phone number from my friend Charles. I'm totally lusting after you, so call me back.

"Hello?"

The sound of a man's deep voice yanked Jeffrey out of his musings. He opened his mouth, but his throat closed as his blood heated. Just that one word in that deep tone caused a rush of arousal to blanket his senses. His cock thickened within his sweatpants so fast his head began to spin.

"Hello?" the man repeated.

"Uh, hi," Jeffrey managed. Clearing his throat quickly, he continued, "Hello. This is Jeffrey Aalders. You, uh—" Jeffrey stalled, then finished, "I'm looking for Mordecai."

"Jeffrey," the man rumbled softly. "Thank you for calling me, Jeffrey. This is Mordecai."

For some reason, the sound of Mordecai pronouncing his name caused Jeffrey's dick to twitch.

Jeffrey grimaced, fighting his reaction. "Uh, sure, Mordecai," he replied, doing his best to keep his voice even. Once again, Jeffrey stalled, his tongue tying. He just didn't know what to say to the man.

"I wish I'd had the fortitude to stay and meet you at the coffee café yesterday," Mordecai stated, his voice deep, soft, and even sounding a little unsure.

Taking that opening, Jeffrey asked, "If you wanted to meet me, why did you leave?"

"My attraction to you threw me for a loop," Mordecai told him. "It was . . . unexpected. And you were there to meet Charles for a date."

Resting the back of his head against the chair's cushion, Jeffrey squinted at the ceiling. "Why was it unexpected? Am I not your normal type?" Another thought struck him. "Or aren't you normally attracted to guys?"

"I'm not usually attracted to anyone," Mordecai answered, obviously being truthful. "That's why it was unexpected."

"Really?" Jeffrey couldn't fathom that. Of course, with the acceptance of homosexuality spreading across the world, he knew other types of sexuality were coming to light. "Are you . . . asexual or . . . something like that?"

"Something like that," Mordecai replied quietly. "I am . . . interested in exploring this with you." He hesitated a few seconds before adding, "But I'm not entirely certain how."

Jeffrey did a mental fist pump. Grinning, he offered, "Well, you're off to a great start. You asked for my phone number."

Mordecai hummed. "And what would be the next step?"

"Well, I suppose—" Jeffrey paused, giving the question a moment of thought, as it deserved. "I suppose there are a couple of different options. Both involve taking the time to talk and get to know each other."

"What options?" Mordecai asked.

"Have you really never dated?" Jeffrey couldn't help but blurt out the question. "Never?"

Mordecai sighed softly. "No, Jeffrey," he answered. "I've never dated." After a second of hesitation, Mordecai asked, "Will you teach me?"

"Does that mean you're a virgin?" The question was out of Jeffrey's mouth before he could censor himself. Wincing, he hissed, "Shit. I shouldn't have asked that. That wasn't appropriate."

No matter how much I want to know the answer.

"I am a virgin," Mordecai told him calmly. A hint of curiosity filled his voice. "Will that be a problem?"

"Oh my god," Jeffrey whispered, disbelief rocking him to the core. "How's that possible? You're sexy as hell."

"Thank you, Jeffrey." Mordecai sounded pleased. "I think you're sexy as well. I wish to slide my fingers into your blond hair, brush it away from your forehead." After letting out a quiet hum, as if imagining doing just that, Mordecai continued, "I would like to trace my fingers along your jaw. When I first saw you, I wondered if I'd feel your stubble or not."

Jeffrey swallowed hard. His dick throbbed in his sweats, and he spread his legs a little to accommodate his aching erection. Pressing the heel of his hand against the base of his shaft, Jeffrey tried to beat back his need to touch himself.

"I'd let you do that," Jeffrey murmured. Thinking of being touched by the big, sexy, virginal man caused a fresh rush of arousal to heat him from the inside out. Jeffrey couldn't help the husky note in his voice when he said, "But my facial hair doesn't grow real fast. I only shave every other morning."

Mordecai hummed, the noise a low deep crooning that went straight to Jeffrey's dick. His cock twitched, pulsing a bead of pre-cum. The man's next word yanked a gasp from

Jeffrey's throat, and his stomach clenched with need.

"I look forward to getting a chance to feel that, Jeffrey."

Letting out a soft groan, Jeffrey murmured, "Shit, Mordecai. That would mean you'd have to be here first thing in the morning."

"That would happen if I spent the night," Mordecai pointed out.

Upon hearing the brazen words, Jeffrey felt his breath catch in his throat. His balls rolled in his sack. He thought of all the things he would like to do to Mordecai that would cause him to stay the night so he would be there first thing in the morning.

"You want to spend the night?" Jeffrey asked.

Shit. How did we go from talking about a date to discussing spending the night?

Jeffrey didn't know, but his body was more than on board with it.

"If you choose me, I would love to spend the night," Mordecai told him enigmatically.

Chuckling, Jeffrey murmured, "I would love to choose you, Mordecai."

A clap of thunder vibrated the house, and a rush of wind flowed through the room, lifting Jeffrey's hair and making the hairs on his nape stand on end.

"Oh, Jeffrey," Mordecai rumbled huskily.

Frowning at the darkness outside his window, Jeffrey did his best to pull himself together. "Damn. I didn't know it was supposed to storm tonight." Even though he hated to do it, he told Mordecai, "I'm sorry. I gotta go check the windows. A breeze just came through here. I must have left a window open."

"Of course, Jeffrey," Mordecai replied. "I understand." After a second, he asked, "May I see you sometime soon? Tomorrow?"

Doing his best to ignore his aching shaft, Jeffrey grinned

as he pushed from his chair. "Yeah. How about you take me to dinner. We can get to know each other better."

Just not the way I really, really *want to get to know you.*

"I'd like that," Mordecai told him. "Will you text me your address, please? I'll pick you up."

"Will do, Mordecai." Jeffrey began walking through the house. "We'll decide on a time, too. See you tomorrow."

"Tomorrow, my *stella guida.*"

Before Jeffrey could ask about the odd endearment, Mordecai ended the call. He set the phone on the end table before walking the house. Except, Jeffrey couldn't find an open window.

Jeffrey's throbbing cock distracted him from the oddity. Settling back in his chair, he shoved his sweats partway down his hips. He gripped his hard cock in one hand, letting out a throaty moan in the process, while cradling his sack with his other palm.

Letting out a deep sigh, Jeffrey closed his eyes. As he jacked his dick and played with his balls, he wondered what kind of package Mordecai sported. Imagining it was the other man's hands on him, Jeffrey sprayed his clean shirt far faster than he could ever remember doing.

Chapter Five

I met my stella guida, creator. Mordecai sat cross-legged on the bed of the cabin the vampire coven was allowing him to borrow. *He unwittingly started our bond.*

With his eyes closed, Mordecai communed with his creator—an ancient being many humans would liken to the god they chose to follow. Long ago, at the dawn of the rise of humans and paranormals—his creator had called angels into being. Angels were tied to their creator until they met their *stella guida* and completed a bond with him or her. They still retained all their abilities to aid humanity, but they were no longer required to return to the realm of their creation to recharge their energy.

I felt the shift in our bond. The creator's voice brushed through his mind, the touch a soft, soothing caress. *Congratulations, my child.*

He knows not what he did. Mordecai hesitated before admitting his concerns. *We have never even spoken in person. What if he comes to regret the decision?*

His creator remained silent for several heartbeats. *Do you intend to do your duty by your* stella guida*?*

Of course! Mordecai didn't understand why his creator would question him on such a thing. *He is my* stella guida. *My guiding star. I'll devote my life to his safety, happiness, and pleasure.* Furrowing his brows, Mordecai thought about that last one. *Once I learn how to do that, anyway.*

When Jeffrey had asked Mordecai if he was a virgin, he'd answered honestly, doing his best to hide his concern. He'd feared that his inexperience would be a strike against him. From the oh-so-quiet sounds that Jeffrey made, noises that Mordecai was certain his human didn't even realize reached him through the line, he'd felt certain that his human was turned on by the knowledge as opposed to the opposite.

Trust in the hands of the Fates, my child. They will not steer you wrong. His creator's words were like a warm balm to Mordecai's worried psyche. *You have been chosen. Share your nature with your human. And remember, you have help available should you need it.*

Letting out a long sigh, Mordecai let go of his worries. *Thank you, creator. I will always endeavor to do you proud.*

And that is the best I could wish for. As Mordecai felt the creator's presence begin to leave him, the ancient being offered a few last words of encouragement. *You and your brethren are attempting to change the world one human at a time, and it is a joy to see. May your future be bright.*

After inhaling slowly, Mordecai let the breath out through pursed lips. He opened his eyes and panned his gaze over the room. The cabin was a one-bedroom that the vampires usually rented to someone who wanted a dude ranch experience. Mordecai had been lucky it had been empty, as a guest had canceled at the last minute.

Mordecai thought perhaps it would be best to bring Jeffrey there to reveal his nature to him. That way, if there were things he didn't know how to answer, or if his human panicked, there were knowledgeable humans around to help him. A number of the vampires were mated to humans, after all.

The more Mordecai thought about it, the more he liked the idea. Plus, he could share some of the guest ranch's activities with his *stella guida*. Mordecai knew from his chat with Charles that Jeffrey worked as a landscaper, and he enjoyed the outdoors.

Perhaps he knows how to horseback ride or would like to try it.

The chuckwagon dinner is also a big hit. There's even fishing in the river that cuts through the property.

So many ways for us to spend time together.

With that idea in mind, Mordecai rose from the bed. He glanced at the clock on the nightstand, seeing it would be time to leave soon. A quick spell had Mordecai clean, refreshed, and dressed in dark jeans, a deep-green button-downed shirt, and a pair of dress boots.

While Mordecai couldn't make something out of nothing—not one being could, not even the creator—he could use a transformation spell. Pretty much, he could make anything from anything else. A nice set of threads was an easy spell.

Mordecai walked out the door of the cabin and paused on the porch. He saw Malakai waiting at the bottom, leaning against the railing. The fellow angel swept his gaze over him, up and down.

"You seem much more settled," Malakai commented with a smile. "Talk to the creator?"

Out of habit, Mordecai glanced around to see who might be within hearing distance.

Malakai smiled. "Relax. Your cabin is the furthest, and no one is about."

Mordecai huffed a sigh even as he nodded. "I did." He headed down the steps slowly, thinking about his next request. Once Mordecai reached the bottom, he faced his fellow angel. "I would like to bring Jeffrey here after our dinner date." Unable to help himself, he rubbed the back of his neck as he muttered, "He chose me last night over the phone. He heard the thunder and felt the wind. I need to explain what's going on."

His eyes widening in obvious surprise, Malakai grasped his upper arms. A wide smile curved his lips. "He *chose* you? That's fantastic!" Malakai stepped forward and wrapped him in a tight hug. "Congratulations, my brother!" With a scoff, he eased his hold and took a step back. "Getting chosen over the phone." He snorted and shook his head even as he smiled largely. "This world never ceases to amaze me."

"Thank you, Malakai," Mordecai murmured, unable to help his own smile. Holding the other angel's gaze, he asked, "And do you think Master Jaymes"—he referred to the master vampire of the coven that ran the dude and guest ranch—"will have issue with me bringing my *stella guida* here to explain . . . everything?"

Malakai smiled as he shook his head. "He'd probably be upset if you *didn't* feel comfortable bringing him here. You'll have plenty of support doing it here." Then he patted Mordecai on the upper arm. "And doing the explanations here is a good idea. Just make certain he has access to a vehicle in case he needs time to flee and come to terms with everything."

"Flee?" Mordecai didn't like the sound of that. Cocking his head, he asked the obvious. "Why would Jeffrey flee?"

Grimacing, Malakai shared, "I've been told that humans can get stuck on the whole *fated* thing." He lifted his fingers and made air quotes. "It can make it difficult for them to accept that a paranormal can truly love him, and that neither one of them are coerced due to"—Malakai paused and squinted toward the heavens for a few heartbeats before meeting Mordecai's gaze once more and finishing—"what they consider a mythological being."

Mordecai nodded slowly. "Okay." He drew the word out slowly. Shaking his head, he tried to understand that. "But humans have so many religions. Their history is ripe with tales of paranormal beings." Mordecai just didn't get it. "Why would they have an issue with a Fate-like being encouraging them to gravitate toward their soul mate?"

Malakai snorted as he rolled his eyes, making Mordecai arch one brow. That was definitely an expression he'd never seen an angel use before. He decided it had to be Murdoch rubbing off on his brother.

Huh. Will I do something similar once I've been with Jeffrey for a time?

For some reason, Mordecai actually looked forward to that.

Go figure.

"One would think a human wouldn't have any problem with it at all," Malakai told him with a shake of his head. With a scoff, he told him, "Considering the literature they have of fated mates and happily-ever-after and stuff like that, you'd think they would welcome a helping hand." Malakai shrugged. "Sadly, they're stuck on this *free will* and *free choice* and how *a fated being is taking that away*." Holding Mordecai's gaze, his fellow angel told him, "Bring Jeffrey here. Explain what we are." Malakai smiled. "Murdoch and I will help, and we'll have a few non-threatening beloveds and shifters on hand so it should be easy for Jeffrey to accept everything."

Mordecai recalled his creator's reminder that he wasn't alone and that he had support.

"Thank you."

Mordecai knew that there was no other appropriate response. Besides, he truly appreciated his fellow angel's offer of help.

May the creator bless me and everything go smoothly.

Pulling up in front of Jeffrey's home, Mordecai admired the beautifully landscaped front yard. The lawn appeared blemish free, and there were flowers popping up in the beds under the front windows. Even the rose bushes were beginning to bud.

It seems my stella guida *enjoys gardening along with landscaping.*

Mordecai appreciated that his guiding star appeared to

enjoy nature so much. Turning his attention to the home itself, he noticed it was in good repair, too. There appeared to be a fresh coat of paint on the pale-blue exterior, and the walkway had been swept clean of debris.

Knowing he needed to stop staring and move up that same walk, Mordecai took a fortifying breath. He couldn't remember ever being so nervous in his life. Mordecai needed the next few hours to go right so very badly.

With another silent prayer to his creator for things to go well, Mordecai exited his borrowed SUV. Once again, vampire master Jaymes Martinez had been more than helpful. While Mordecai could have transformed a stand of trees into a vehicle, the vampire had assured him that he didn't need to expend his power on something so trivial.

Mordecai would never counter a gift from the master of the coven, so he'd accepted.

Shoving the keys into the pocket of his jacket, Mordecai strode swiftly toward the door. He took the two steps in one. On the small porch, he pushed the doorbell button and immediately heard the chime ring within the home.

A few seconds later, Mordecai's sensitive hearing allowed him to pick up the tread of approaching footsteps. His heart rate sped up in his chest. He felt sweat begin to bead on his lower back as anticipation surged through him.

Mordecai's breath caught in his throat when Jeffrey opened the door, and his *stella guida* stood before him. His human was just as gorgeous as he remembered. Every impulse within him urged him to reach out and grab the man, to pull him close and tuck him within the safety of his arms and wings.

Barely resisting, Mordecai's fingers twitched at his sides. "Hi, Jeffrey," he managed to rumble. "You look . . . amazing."

The wide smile Jeffrey graced him with caused butterflies

to bump in Mordecai's belly, and his blood heated in his veins, quickly flowing south.

For the first time ever, Mordecai stood before a human with a hard-on, and he had no idea what to do about it.

Chapter Six

Even with Mordecai standing on the porch, which was a step below the house entrance, he still topped Jeffrey, forcing him to look up to meet the larger man's gaze. Jeffrey's breath caught in his throat upon seeing the appreciative heat in Mordecai's exotic aqua-colored eyes. Jeffrey's pulse raced, and he grinned upon hearing the handsome man's compliment.

"Thanks," Jeffrey replied, somehow finding his tongue. "You look pretty amazing yourself."

Jeffrey couldn't help checking the man out. His dark jeans appeared to be molded to his legs, showcasing muscular thighs. The deep-green button-down shirt he saw between the flaps of the jacket accentuated his pectorals. It also brought out the color in Mordecai's eyes.

"Thank you," Mordecai murmured, his deep voice sounding even better in person. His fingers twitched at his sides, and his expression grew intense. For all the world, Mordecai looked like he wanted to grab Jeffrey and pull him close. Then he cleared his throat and took a step backward. "Are you ready to go?"

Too bad. Maybe it makes me a slut, but if he'd grabbed me, I woulda led him into the house. Dinner can wait. Or we could order in and eat nude.

For an instant, Mordecai's eyes widened just a smidge. Then the man glanced away.

Jeffrey wondered at that, but when Mordecai returned his attention to him and offered a hesitant-looking smile, he dismissed it. Returning the man's smile with another of his own, he exited his house. After making certain it was locked, Jeffrey followed Mordecai down his walkway to the newer model SUV sitting in the driveway.

"So, where are we going?" Jeffrey asked. When Mordecai opened the passenger door for him, he felt a rush of warmth at the thoughtful gesture. "Thanks."

Jeffrey understood that it was a sign of respect and in no way meant that he was lesser than Mordecai.

"I'm here visiting, so I asked my friend, Malakai, for a suggestion," Mordecai told him. "He recommended The Wagoneer steakhouse." Standing in the passenger doorway, he asked, "Is that okay with you?"

Nodding, Jeffrey told him, "I haven't been there in a while, but I do like that place." The last time he'd been had been with a few friends in celebration of one of their wives finally getting pregnant. "Their onion strings are delicious."

"We'll have to get some," Mordecai replied easily.

Once again, Jeffrey thought Mordecai would touch him in some way. The bigger man lifted his hand as if to place it on Jeffrey's thigh. After freezing a second, clearly hesitating, Mordecai took a step backward and closed the door.

Hmmm. Why is he hesitating?

Then it occurred to Jeffrey.

He claimed to be a virgin. No wonder he's unsure.

Jeffrey realized that, in the touching department, he would have to make the first move.

I can do that.

Once Mordecai slid behind the wheel and started them moving, Jeffrey rested his left forearm on the center console. He leaned toward the bigger man. When Mordecai glanced his way, Jeffrey smiled at him.

Mordecai smiled back before returning his attention to the road.

When they stopped at a light, Jeffrey reached over and

touched Mordecai's jacket-clad upper arm. "You said you're visiting." Jeffrey felt Mordecai's thick bicep tighten under his fingers, but he didn't comment on it. "Where do you call home?"

Just how long-distance of a relationship would I have to have to keep this guy?

Damn. Getting ahead of yourself again, Jeffrey.

The light turned green, and Mordecai started them forward, glancing at the GPS embedded in the dash. "I live in a different realm that's far away from here," he told him. Before Jeffrey could question the odd statement, Mordecai glanced his way once more and told him, "I intend to move here. Do you like living here?"

"Yeah, I like the area," Jeffrey replied with a nod. *That's a relief.* "Are you moving because of your job? What do you do?"

Mordecai opened his mouth, hesitating. His brows furrowed. After a glance toward Jeffrey again, Mordecai returned his attention to the road.

"Sweet creator, this is more difficult than I imagined," Mordecai whispered with a shake of his head.

Confused, Jeffrey straightened in his seat. "What's difficult?" he questioned. He narrowed his eyes as he stared at Mordecai. "Do you do something illegal, Mordecai?"

To Jeffrey's surprise, Mordecai chuckled even as he shook his head. "No, most definitely not."

Mordecai swallowed so hard his Adam's apple bobbed. Then he nodded once, as if coming to a decision. When Mordecai pulled the car over to the side of the road, worry filled Jeffrey.

Is Mordecai calling a halt to our date?

"I'm not calling a halt to our date, Jeffrey," Mordecai told him, as if he'd said the words out loud. He turned and pinned him with a serious look. "I want to answer every question you have, but there's so much to explain." With a shake of his head, Mordecai reached over and placed his hand over Jeffrey's. "Some of what I have to say will sound . . . unbelievable. Maybe confusing, and the cab of an SUV is not the place to have the conversation. Nor is sitting at a table in a busy restaurant." Mordecai squeezed Jeffrey's hand lightly. "May we go somewhere private instead?"

When Mordecai had placed his hand over Jeffrey's, it had sent a cascade of warm tingles up his arm. The hairs had stood on end. The wonderful sensation was making it difficult to think, let alone follow Mordecai's sentences. Jeffrey wondered what Mordecai's wonderful palms would feel like stroking other parts of his body.

Still, Jeffrey realized he'd been asked a question. "Private?" Even though he'd fantasized about dragging Mordecai into his home instead of going to dinner, being asked outright to be alone with an absolute stranger caused a red flag to wave in his mind. Unable to help the wariness in his tone, Jeffrey asked, "Where were you thinking?"

"I told you about my friend, Malakai," Mordecai replied, squeezing Jeffrey's hand once more. "He lives at Rolling Meadows Ranch up north. Do you know it?"

Jeffrey nodded. "I've heard of it. Never been there, though." He knew the place was about forty-five minutes north and was a cattle ranch. The place was pretty upscale and offered dude ranch experiences. "I, uh, looked into it once, but it was too rich for my blood."

"Well, now you have a chance to check it out for free," Mordecai told him with a smile. "I'm staying in a cabin up there. I'll order dinner to be delivered, and I'll share everything about me that you could possibly want to know." Then his brows furrowed, and once again, he seemed to know what Jeffrey had been thinking. "And you are completely safe with me, Jeffrey. I would never hurt you."

"How do you seem to guess when I'm worried about

something?" Jeffrey asked, unable to help himself. "It's like . . . like you can read my mind or something."

Mordecai rubbed his thumb over Jeffrey's pulse point, sending a fresh wave of tingles up his arm. "Or something," he murmured softly. With a pointed glance at where he touched him, Mordecai told him, "When you're upset, your pulse speeds up."

"Oh." Jeffrey nodded. "That makes sense." Then, deciding to indulge his curiosity, he told him, "Okay. Let's check out this dude ranch."

"Thank you, my *stella guida,*" Mordecai rumbled, a clearly pleased smile curving his lips. His aqua eyes glimmered in the evening light. "Your trust is not misplaced."

Jeffrey nodded slowly even as he asked, "What's *stella guida* mean?" He recalled Mordecai calling him that the prior evening on the phone.

Mordecai returned the SUV to the road, but he didn't release Jeffrey. "*Stella guida* means guiding star," he told him softly. After a glance at him, he stated, "That is what you mean to me. You have given me something I can never repay." Mordecai squeezed Jeffrey's hand once more while flashing a smile his way.

Cocking his head, Jeffrey thought about that. It was an odd endearment. His explanation confused him, too.

"Gave you something?" Jeffrey repeated slowly. "I don't know about that." Then a thought clicked, and he shifted in his seat while clearing his throat. "Uh, do you mean a, uh . . . a sex drive?"

With a smile curving his lips, Mordecai shrugged one shoulder. "Although I imagine that'll be a heady perk, no."

"Then what?" Jeffrey pressed, confusion filling him.

Mordecai hummed softly and cast another glance his way. "It goes back to when you asked about my job as well as where I'm from," he rumbled in a soft voice. "My brethren and I, we . . . are tasked with . . . helping others in certain ways."

Jeffrey could tell that Mordecai was struggling with how to explain. The streetlights played off the angles of his aristocratic features, showing how his brows were furrowed. Jeffrey even made out the tense line of his jaw and the pinch of his lips.

Mmmm, I'd love to taste those lips. I wonder if I could kiss that tension away.

Mordecai blinked quickly as his nostrils flared. He cut a quick glance Jeffrey's way, revealing the heat in his eyes, before he returned his focus to the road. His wide torso expanded and contracted as he took several deep breaths.

Damn. Sometimes, it really feels like he can read my mind. Is that one of the odd things he wants to explain? Except, how could something like that even be possible?

Unable to help himself, Jeffrey brought up a mental image of what he guessed Mordecai's chest looked like. He imagined himself licking and nipping over the large man's collarbone. Jeffrey wanted to scrape his teeth along his firm flesh. He wondered what he would taste like, how he would respond as he suckled one of Mordecai's hard nipples.

Will Mordecai shiver when I scrape my fingernails along his sides, across the dips of his abdominals, or when I dip my thumbs beneath the waist of his jeans to tease into the grooves of his hips?

Predictably, Jeffrey's dick reacted to his thoughts. He went hard as nails in seconds. His balls felt heavy and swollen, and he fought his need to adjust himself.

What truly fascinated Jeffrey, however, was the way Mordecai's eyes widened once more. His chest heaved, his nostrils flared, and he parted his lips on a soft pant. His hand holding Jeffrey's twitched.

"You can read my mind," Jeffrey whispered in shock and awe. Maybe a little trepidation, too. "Can't you?"

Mordecai swallowed so hard his Adam's apple bobbed

before he rasped, "Yes." He cut a glance Jeffrey's way as he told him, "If someone's feelings on what they're thinking about are strong enough, I can pick up on those thoughts."

Jeffrey shook his head slowly, disbelief creeping in. "How is that possible?" He'd never heard of such a thing. Well, not outside of science fiction or fantasy movies or books.

"I didn't want to be driving when I explained this," Mordecai answered heavily. His brows furrowed, and his expression turned pensive. Cutting a look Jeffrey's way, Mordecai almost sounded pleading when he said, "Can we wait until we get to the ranch, please? There's so much to explain."

Jeffrey recalled Mordecai saying that once before. He figured, if he was to truly give this guy a chance, he would need to allow him said chance to explain. Mordecai was right that a moving vehicle wasn't really the place for it.

"Okay," Jeffrey agreed. "At the ranch." After a second of hesitation, he added the caveat, "But I want the keys to your SUV."

He needed an escape plan . . . just in case.

Momma didn't raise no fool.

Mordecai winced even as he nodded. "I understand your need."

"Thanks."

Releasing his hand, Mordecai pulled his cell phone from his inside pocket. After hitting a button, he lifted it to his ear. Someone must have answered.

"I'm bringing Jeffrey to the ranch. We skipped dinner." Mordecai paused for a few seconds, then answered, "He started asking questions I couldn't answer in a public place." After another few seconds, Mordecai murmured, "Thank you, Malakai. Can we have a meal brought to the cabin? We're about fifteen minutes out."

After Mordecai thanked his friend again, he hung up the phone and put it back into his jacket pocket.

To Jeffrey's pleasure, Mordecai once again took his hand.

Chapter Seven

Mordecai hadn't been able to control his reaction when Jeffrey had begun mentally broadcasting his desires. His body had responded just from the images he was getting from his human. When his *stella guida* had asked a straightforward question, Mordecai hadn't been able—or willing—to lie to him.

To his relief, Jeffrey hadn't freaked out.

Well, not yet, anyway.

Mordecai had understood Jeffrey's request for an avenue of escape. Eventually, he would have to tell his human that, since he'd started their bond, he would be able to track him down no matter where he went. They were connected on a soul-deep level.

And when I complete the bond, Jeffrey will develop some of my gifts.

So much to explain.

They rode in silence, but Mordecai found it companionable as opposed to awkward. He continued to hold Jeffrey's hand, enjoying the simple interaction. His human's palm and fingers were work-roughened and felt good against his own callouses.

Arriving at the ranch, Mordecai turned the SUV into the driveway. "I understand this is a beautiful place," he murmured, glancing at the landscape hidden in shadows. "I haven't done much exploring, yet, but I look forward to doing that with you."

"And the owners of the ranch don't care that you're

bringing a guest onto their property?" Jeffrey furrowed his brows as he glanced from Mordecai to the window and back again. "Aren't there additional fees for more people and waivers and shit at a place like this?"

Mordecai frowned. "Waivers?"

"Yeah." Jeffrey focused on him. "Didn't you sign a waiver?" When Mordecai hesitated, Jeffrey pressed, "You know. A form indicating that if you get injured, you won't sue them?"

Shaking his head, Mordecai admitted, "I did not." As he took the right fork in the driveway, passing the barns and other cabins, he mused, "Perhaps for humans that would be necessary."

"Humans?" Jeffrey jumped on Mordecai's slip. "Uh, care to explain that?"

Mordecai nodded once. "You asked how I could possibly read someone's mind." He spotted Malakai and Murdoch sitting on the pair of rockers on the porch of his borrowed cabin. Once Mordecai had parked the SUV and shut it off, he pulled the keys from the ignition. Turning to Jeffrey, he offered them to his *stella guida.* Mordecai held the human's gaze as he took them and murmured, "Jeffrey, my *stella guida,* I am not human." Still holding his attention, Mordecai used his free hand to indicate his friends on the porch. "They are not human, either."

With his keen eyesight, Mordecai saw the blood drain from Jeffrey's face. His jaw clenched. His Adam's apple bobbed. When Jeffrey licked his lips, Mordecai followed the movement, wanting very much to engage in his first kiss.

The scent of fear and uncertainty filling the cab stayed his desire.

"Not human," Jeffrey whispered hoarsely. "So what are you?" His attention darted to the pair who were now standing on the porch. "What are they?"

"You are completely safe with me, Jeffrey," Mordecai stated instead of answering. "Completely safe with them. None of us would ever hurt you."

"You didn't answer the question," Jeffrey accused.

Shaking his head, Mordecai admitted, "No, I didn't." He stared into his human's eyes, seeing the fear there. "I can scent your fear, your uncertainty. It pains me that you think I would ever hurt you." With a sigh, Mordecai eased away from Jeffrey and opened his door. He slipped from the vehicle and stood in the doorway, meeting Jeffrey's gaze once more. "Will you come inside, Jeffrey? Will you share a meal with me as I explain what I am?" Mordecai glanced toward his friends for a second. "What we are? How we're different but absolutely no threat to you?"

Or will you run away?

Mordecai kept that last question to himself. He could see the desire to flee in Jeffrey's expressive green eyes. As tempting as it was to just grab Jeffrey and carry him inside, Mordecai knew this had to be his human's choice.

Watching Jeffrey inhale deeply, then let it out through pursed lips, Mordecai couldn't seem to get a read on his thoughts. Perhaps they were too scrambled. He could guess there was a fair amount of disbelief, denial, and even a need for Mordecai to be lying to him.

He waited.

After a long moment, Jeffrey slowly nodded. "You promise I'm not in any danger?"

"You have my word, Jeffrey," Mordecai stated. Touching his own chest, he added, "I would lay down my life for yours."

Jeffrey nodded. "Okay."

To Mordecai's relief—and absolute joy—Jeffrey opened his car door and climbed out. Mordecai shut his own door and rounded the hood. He smiled at Jeffrey when his human joined him. His *stella guida*'s return smile was tentative, but it was there.

I'll take it.

Turning, Mordecai indicated the pair standing on the porch. "The one on the left is Malakai. The right is Murdoch." He hesitated, then added, "They are a bonded couple."

"Bonded couple?" Jeffrey repeated, glancing between them, then back at Mordecai. "What's that mean?"

"Paranormal jargon for partners," Murdoch replied with a smile. "Nice to meet you, Jeffrey. Mordecai's description doesn't do you justice. You smell delicious."

Jeffrey tensed. "Huh?"

Malakai frowned at his vampire. "My *stella guida,* why did you have to comment like that?" With a shake of his head, he returned his attention to Jeffrey. "Murdoch is a vampire. He likes the smell of your blood." Then he narrowed his eyes at his lover. "Although he'd never sample Jeffrey."

Murdoch growled softly as he leveled a hungry look Malakai's way. "You know you're the only one I'll ever drink from again, my beloved."

"And you'd best not forget that," Malakai grumbled, wrapping his arm around Murdoch and pulling him close.

"Love you all possessive," Murdoch crooned right before Malakai took his mouth in a deep kiss.

Gaping, Jeffrey turned his attention to Mordecai. "What just happened?" he whispered. After a furtive glance toward the couple again, he squeaked, "Vampire? Y-You're a vampire?"

"No, my *stella guida,*" Mordecai replied. "Murdoch is a vampire." Taking a chance, he rested his palm against Jeffrey's back. "Malakai and I are something else." While he felt Jeffrey tense beneath his hand, his human didn't pull away. Guiding his *stella guida* toward the porch, moving around the making-out couple, Mordecai added, "And as I said.

They are a bonded couple. Vampires cannot drink the blood of anyone else once they meet their beloved." Realizing Jeffrey wouldn't know what that was, he quickly added, "Soul mate. Uh, a vampire's beloved is similar to our kind's *stella guida.*"

"And you are?" Jeffrey pressed, glancing at him with furrowed brows.

Opening the cabin door, Mordecai led the way inside, flipping on the light switch to the main room as he went. Knowing he shouldn't put it off any longer, he smiled at Jeffrey as he closed the door. In the relative safety of the cabin, Mordecai lowered his glamour, allowing his wings to appear.

Upon seeing Jeffrey's jaw sag open and his eyes widen, Mordecai murmured, "I'm an angel." After a second of hesitation, he added, "So is Malakai."

"Holy shit!"

Jeffrey's whispered words barely reached Mordecai as he stumbled backward a couple of steps. He glanced around swiftly, and Mordecai feared he was searching for a place to run. Instead, Jeffrey staggered to the loveseat and collapsed upon it.

Gaping, Jeffrey continued to stare at Mordecai.

Mordecai slowly moved toward Jeffrey, needing to be close to his *stella guida*. His heart hammered in his chest as he saw his human tense. Stopping a few feet in front of him, Mordecai lowered to his knees, putting them close to the same height.

Tentatively, Mordecai moved his hands toward Jeffrey. He rested them on his *stella guida*'s knees. His human trembled under his touch, but he didn't pull away.

"Take slow deep breaths, Jeffrey," Mordecai encouraged. Sliding his hands up his human's legs just a little, he massaged his lower thigh soothingly. "You're okay. You're perfectly safe."

Nodding slowly, Jeffrey licked his lips. He roved his gaze all over Mordecai, as if trying to figure out where to look first. His attention snagged on Mordecai's wings, and he clenched his fingers into fists on the cushions next to his legs.

If Mordecai had to guess, Jeffrey was barely able to stop himself from reaching out to touch.

That won't do.

"You're welcome to touch me, Jeffrey," Mordecai encouraged, sliding his hands up higher as he folded his wings forward, closer, in invitation. "In fact, I'd like it if you did."

Mordecai marveled at the strong, toned muscles hidden beneath the jeans Jeffrey wore. He couldn't help how husky his voice sounded. The idea of Jeffrey running his hands over his wings sent a tremble through him.

As a general rule, angels were careful of their wings. While the glamour spell hid their wings, they *were* still there. They didn't particularly like them being touched by others, however, and took great care where they sat or stood in a room.

But for my stella guida *to touch them . . . I know it'll feel exquisite.*

"Angels are real," Jeffrey murmured, as if needing to say it out loud to convince himself. He lifted a trembling right hand toward Mordecai's wing. "I can't believe this is real."

Then Jeffrey leaned forward and rested his fingertips on the top of Mordecai's left wing. He skimmed his hands along the feathers, petting him. His look of disbelief turned to awe, and he lifted his hand only to do it again.

Mordecai practically vibrated. Just as he'd expected, feeling Jeffrey's touch caused tingles to erupt along his skin. The hairs on his nape stood on end. Even his gut clenched as fire settled in his groin, and his erection throbbed behind his fly.

Could I orgasm from him petting my wings?

While Mordecai would love to find out, he didn't feel it was appropriate in that moment. Especially since, at that second, his cabin's door opened. Snapping his attention to those who entered, Mordecai instinctively glamoured his wings, which caused Jeffrey to snap his hand away.

"Relax." Malakai entered with Murdoch following. "It's just us." Their lips were kiss-swollen, and they both sported satisfied expressions. "We brought dinner."

They carried covered trays, and Mordecai wondered where they'd gotten them. Except, that didn't concern him the most.

Scenting the unmistakable aroma of spent seed, Mordecai grumbled, "Be sure to wash your hands before touching anything."

Malakai appeared a bit sheepish even as Murdoch laughed.

"Fangs," Jeffrey whispered, drawing Mordecai's attention.

Mordecai massaged Jeffrey's thighs once more. "Yes, Murdoch has fangs." When his *stella guida* snapped his attention to him, he shrugged. "Vampire, remember?"

Jeffrey nodded in an absent manner even as his brows furrowed. "Why'd you tell them to wash their hands?" Rubbing the back of his neck, he asked, "Should I wash my hands?"

Grimacing, Mordecai admitted, "At some point after kissing and before entering the cabin, they—" Mordecai paused, uncertain how blunt to be.

Murdoch had no such hang-up. "It was *during* kissing," the vampire claimed from where he stood Malakai, who was at the sink. Waggling his brows, he told them, "We stumbled into the trees, opened our pants, and frotted to completion." Murdoch sighed deeply as he cast a satisfied look on Malakai. "And, gods, it felt amazing." Malakai dried his hands while pinning Murdoch with a satisfied stare, and Murdoch softly claimed, "Always does, my beloved."

Mordecai suddenly felt like a voyeur. He turned his attention to Jeffrey, who was eyeing the pair with amusement.

Huh. That's interesting.

"A bonded vampire can't drink from anyone but his partner?"

Upon hearing Jeffrey's softly stated question, Mordecai nodded. "Correct."

Jeffrey scoffed as he turned his attention back to the pair. "So, you made that comment about me smelling good to wind Malakai up, so you could get a little action."

As Murdoch washed his hands, he winked at Jeffrey. "Hell, yeah, man." His expression turned predatory as he refocused on Malakai. "Nothin' better than my man hot and bothered for me."

Barking a laugh, Jeffrey smirked. "Guess paranormal couples aren't all that different than human ones."

Mordecai hoped Jeffrey still felt that way after he explained that there were indeed differences between them.

Chapter Eight

Jeffrey figured he was sort of in shock. His mind reeled with all the revelations of the last fifteen minutes. They'd moved to the table to eat, and Mordecai's friends had helped explain different paranormal creatures.

Angels, vampires, and shifters, oh my!

Yep. Definitely a little in shock.

When Jeffrey had asked how Mordecai would remove the jacket that he was wearing, considering his wings and all—*which are totally stunning. Just wow*—he'd nearly fallen out of his chair when the jacket had just . . . disappeared.

As Jeffrey stabbed his fork into a perfectly done medium-rare piece of steak, he eyed Murdoch. "So, you're a vampire, but you eat real food."

Murdoch nodded as he chewed. After he'd swallowed, he explained, "Most myths about the paranormal are full of ridiculous inaccuracies." He put down his fork and began ticking off his fingers. "Vampires eat food. We don't turn into bats. We're not allergic to garlic or holy water. Shifters don't need a full moon to change. Demons aren't the spawn of the devil out to destroy lives. Angels don't fight demons." When Murdoch ran out of fingers, he began flicking up the ones on his other hand. "The Four Horsemen of the Apocalypse aren't going to usher in the end of the world. Gargoyles are not evil deranged creatures."

"Whoa, whoa!" Jeffrey held up both hands, palms out, his fork dangling between his thumb and pointer finger. "You're fryin' my brain, man." Shaking his head, he frowned at the vampire. "Shit. Demons and gargoyles and the Four Horsemen? What the hell?"

Mordecai reached over and gripped one of Jeffrey's hands. "Just relax, Jeffrey," he rumbled, squeezing lightly as he pulled it toward him. After bussing a kiss to his palm, Mordecai murmured, "We don't need to explain all the particulars right away. There is so much. It'll come in time."

Jeffrey nodded, liking the sound of that. He knew he was already overwhelmed. Blowing out a breath, Jeffrey smiled at the beautiful man—angel—sitting next to him.

"Sounds good," Jeffrey replied softly, as he swept his gaze over Mordecai's aristocratic features. His initial thought of him looking like a warrior of old had ended up truer than ever. "Never would have imagined things like you and"—he waved toward Murdoch, then the ranch at large, since he now knew it was a vampire coven with some shifters thrown in—"could ever possibly have existed."

"The world is more complex than the average human could possibly imagine," Mordecai responded with a nod. "And the secret is sacred. Anonymity is the paranormals' greatest ally." His expression grew grave. "You can never tell a soul about us."

Chuckling, Jeffrey grinned at the group's serious expressions. "Who would I tell?" When they exchanged looks, his mirth faded. "Okay. I promise not to tell a soul. I imagine the average person would report me to the men in the white coats." Jeffrey glanced between the men. While Mordecai's brows furrowed as if in confusion, Murdoch smirked, and Malakai winced. "But you're not so sure about that. Are you?"

"Just like in any society, there are fringe groups that wish to subjugate those different than them. There are small pockets of humans that know about us," Murdoch revealed with a sigh. "Some use religion as their basis for hunting us.

Others want shifter pelts or vampire teeth or gargoyle heads as trophies. Some are just assholes."

"Then there are the scientists who want to study us." Malakai picked up the explanation. "Do experiments on us. Figure out a way to give some of our abilities to soldiers, making super soldiers, that sort of thing."

Jeffrey grimaced as he shook his head. "That's terrible."

He couldn't imagine these beautiful creatures trapped in a cage. Just the image of someone plucking their wing feathers as trophies made him see red. Bowing his head, he breathed deeply.

No one will ever hurt Mordecai on my watch.

Mordecai lifted Jeffrey's hand, which he still held, to his lips once more. "Thank you for caring," he murmured, having obviously caught the thought.

Malakai smiled fondly at him, probably having heard his vehement thought, too.

Sliding his fork through his mashed potatoes and gravy, Murdoch winked at him. "On to happier thoughts." Before slipping the food into his mouth, the vampire stated, "Let's skip to the good bit."

"Good bit?"

Good grief. More information?

"There always seems to be more," Mordecai commented. Holding Jeffrey's gaze, he added, "I think Murdoch is referring to the, uh, well—" He paused, stumbling over his words. With a glance at the others, Mordecai resumed, "I'm completely devoted to you, Jeffrey. Your happiness, safety, enjoyment." Mordecai began gently massaging his hand. "I'll do everything in my power to make our eternal lives together to be filled with love and bliss."

"Eternal lives?" Jeffrey whispered, staring at Mordecai as shock rolled through him . . . again. "W-We'll live . . . forever?"

"While an angel can be killed, barring any sort of fight or

injury, yes. We'll live forever," Mordecai answered obviously being honest once more. "When we finish our bond, our life-threads will entwine, and you will live as long as I do. So, forever."

"Holy shit," Jeffrey squeaked. Gaping, he glanced at the others, who wore worried expressions. Snapping his attention back to Mordecai, Jeffrey saw the angel's concerned expression. "Why the hell would you offer something like that to me?" He didn't get it. "I'm no one special."

"You are *extremely* special," Mordecai countered, gazing at him earnestly. "You are my *stella guida*. The one human on this plane of existence that I can bond with." Rubbing small circles over Jeffrey's pulse point with his thumb, Mordecai added, "I feel beyond grateful that the Fates have finally put you in my path."

"The Fates?" Jeffrey decided things just kept getting weirder and weirder, and he'd had just about enough. Shaking his head, he murmured, "Forget I asked that. I don't care right now."

Jeffrey opened his mouth, then closed it again. He just didn't know what to ask anymore.

Murdoch leaned forward, resting his forearms on the table. "The good bit I was actually referring to was the epic sex." He smirked as he waggled his eyebrows. "Once you teach Mordecai here what you like"—Murdoch used his steak knife to point at the angel in question—"then you'll have epic sex. Plus, because a paranormal's sex drive is higher than the average human's, yours will increase to match. Then you'll have that epic sex often." With a wink, the vampire stated, "Why do you think I wanted to step away and get some? The feel of your soul mate's shaft filling you is probably going to become a craving. You'll want to feel him stretch you and flood your ass with his cream all the damn time."

Gaping once more, Jeffrey felt his face heat up. He didn't consider himself a prude by any means, but he'd never had anyone speak so bluntly about fucking in front of him. His embarrassment was mixed with a healthy dose of lust, as desire surged through him upon thinking of Mordecai laying him out and fucking him senseless.

Jeffrey's cock swelled to hard and aching so fast he nearly swayed in his seat from blood loss. His chest hitched as he struggled to catch his breath. Even his nipples beaded as he thought about what it would feel like to have Mordecai's hands on him.

"Well, Jeffrey likes the sound of that," Murdoch stated on a husky chuckle. He patted Malakai's arm. "Maybe we should head out so they can finish their bond." Waggling his eyebrows, Murdoch urged, "Don't think about it too much, Jeffrey. Accept the gift that's been given to you, and let Mordecai pleasure you all night long."

Nothing had ever sounded so fantastic.

Except, Jeffrey knew there was one more important bit he needed to know. "You talk about bonding. What is that? And what's it mean for me?" Meeting Mordecai's hopeful gaze, Jeffrey added, "And for you?"

"All good things," Murdoch assured as he rose from his seat. Patting Jeffrey on the shoulder, he picked up his empty plate. "This is one of those things that it's better if you just don't overthink it. We know that most humans don't believe in a soul mate, someone designed to be a damn near perfect match." Murdoch shrugged, his smile turning wry. "But to us, well, we look forward to finding that special someone from the day we learn of it. Living a long life does have its drawbacks. Finding our soul mate gives us someone to share that long life with. This is a blessing for Mordecai. Don't ever think otherwise."

Jeffrey nodded slowly as he realized just how serious the

vampire had become. During the course of the evening, he'd thought of the man as laid-back, relaxed, and a bit of a jokester. Hearing the solemness in his tone made Jeffrey realize that there was a lot more to the friendly guy than he'd first thought.

It also reinforced how serious this was.

As Jeffrey watched Murdoch and Malakai clear their dishes and place them on the platter they'd used to bring the food, he let his mind spin through everything he'd learned in the past hour. There was a lot—new species residing right alongside humans. Different realms where even more beings existed.

Holy hell. Even what humans considered gods were truly real, including the Olympians.

Talk about crazy shit!

When the door closed behind the pair, leaving him alone with Mordecai, Jeffrey felt a wash of nerves flood him. He felt the angel massage his palm once more. It was soothing and stimulating all at the same time, sending tingles up his arm and making the hairs there stand on end.

"We can wait, if you need more time," Mordecai offered softly, his expression pensive. "I know this has been a lot to take in. To accept."

Jeffrey met Mordecai's gaze squarely. "This is like marriage, isn't it?"

How had he missed that before?

To Jeffrey's surprise, Mordecai shook his head. "No, this is not like human's idea of marriage," he told him, his deep voice soft and certain. "This is so much *more*. Our lives will be entwined. You'll become my entire world, my reason for existence, my *stella guida*, my guiding star. I will live to see to your needs."

"That sounds a little one-sided, Mordecai," Jeffrey pointed out. "What about *your* needs?"

Mordecai smiled, his aqua eyes taking on a twinkle. "Ah,

but you see, by pleasing you, I'm following my nature. That makes me happy." Then he sobered as he added, "There's no chance of divorce in this. Once we finish our bond, we will be as one." Mordecai's brows furrowed, and a hint of a growl filled his voice. "You saw how jealous Malakai became when Murdoch teased him about your scent. Bonded paranormals are jealous bastards, so I've seen. I will never have another, and in the future, I'll be the only one for you, too."

Jeffrey couldn't help but smile back at Mordecai upon learning that. "I'm a one-man kind of guy, so that works out perfect." He couldn't imagine ever wanting someone else. After all, Mordecai was about damn perfect. "So, how do we finish this bond you speak of?" Cocking his head, he furrowed his brows. "How'd you start it, anyway?"

He didn't know how he felt about Mordecai starting their bond without his permission, but he knew he would get over it. After all, what was done was done.

To Jeffrey's surprise, Mordecai told him, "I didn't start our bond. You did, my *stella guida*." The angel must have realized how that confused him, for he explained, "Last night when you told me that you chose me. You remember the thunderclap and wind? You thought you'd left a window open?"

Jeffrey nodded, recalling that, although he hadn't been able to find one.

"Well, those simple words coupled with my name was all that was needed," Mordecai shared. "You accepted me, chose me, and to our species, that was all it took to begin the bond."

"Huh." Jeffrey scoffed softly. Then he shrugged before smiling at Mordecai. "Okay. And how do we finish it?"

Mordecai swallowed hard, his Adam's apple bobbing. After clearing his throat, he rumbled huskily, "Sex, Jeffrey."

Then Mordecai reached over and touched where Jeffrey's neck met his shoulder. "And I'll give you a claiming bite here."

"A bite?" Jeffrey winced. He wasn't much into pain with his pleasure.

Offering one slow nod, Mordecai claimed, "It'll make you orgasm." His expression turned predatory. "In fact, I've heard that partners beg for it over and over."

Jeffrey's breath caught in his chest.

Well, boy howdy!

Grinning broadly, Jeffrey whispered, "Let's get this party started."

Chapter Nine

For one heartbeat, two, confusion flooded Mordecai. He wasn't certain what that meant. Upon seeing Jeffrey's grin, it clicked.

"Y-You want to . . . with me?" Mordecai felt his cheeks heat.

Good grief. I can't even say it.

Jeffrey slowly rose to his feet, leveling a heated gaze upon Mordecai. "Yes, my angel," he crooned huskily. "I would like to experience this bonding with you."

Rising, Mordecai groaned softly. A shiver worked down his spine, settling in his balls, when he heard his human claiming him. His dick ached behind the fly of his jeans. The change in position offered him a bit more room, but he still wasn't comfortable.

How do men deal with this on a regular basis?

Mordecai figured he would end up finding out. He couldn't imagine not responding to his *stella guida.* The man was just too tempting.

Holding out his hand, Mordecai fought back a tremble. "I will need guidance," he admitted. "I have never."

"I still find that absolutely mind-blowing," Jeffrey admitted as he placed his hand in Mordecai's. "You're a stunning man, Mordecai, even without those gorgeous feathered wings."

"Angels don't have a sex drive until they meet their *stella guida,* Jeffrey," Mordecai reminded his human. His soon-to-be lover's words made him wonder if the man didn't believe him. "Until I spotted you in that coffee café, I'd never experienced arousal." Seeing Jeffrey's brows shoot up, Mordecai admitted, "It was . . . thrilling and startling and a little scary all at once."

Jeffrey smiled up at him, his green eyes gleaming in the lamplight. "I imagine it was." Taking the lead, his human led the way into the bedroom as he stated, "Experiencing something so intense for the first time after . . . how many years?"

Mordecai shrugged, admitting, "I don't know. Our creator made us at the dawn of man. I've always been here."

Nodding, Jeffrey murmured, "Right." Pausing at the foot of the bed, he raked his heated gaze over Mordecai. "So, you use magick to clothe yourself." Jeffrey rested his hands on his pectorals. "Can you just remove the shirt? I want to peel away the rest."

Sucking in a sharp breath, Mordecai did as his *stella guida* requested. A second later, his human's hands were on his skin, and he was moving them, gliding his palms over his pectorals. His nipples immediately tightened, and tingles trickled across his chest.

"Jeffrey," Mordecai whispered, his voice sounding far harsher than he'd ever heard it.

Jeffrey didn't seem concerned. He smiled up at Mordecai. "Your skin is so smooth and soft over your hard muscles. It makes my blood burn to know that I'm the only one who'll ever get to touch you like this."

Mordecai groaned, lifting his hands. For a second, he hesitated before cradling Jeffrey's jaws with his palms. "I wish to taste your lips," he admitted softly, peering into Jeffrey's deep green eyes. "May I?"

"Any time you want, Mordecai," Jeffrey responded with a smile. "You never have to ask. You'll always have my permission."

Letting out another quiet moan, Mordecai gave in to temptation. He settled his lips over Jeffrey's. He'd seen enough people kiss over the millennia, but it still took him a few seconds to get the coordination right.

Sliding his lips against Jeffrey's soft mouth, Mordecai felt a warmth flood his veins. He eased his lips apart and flicked out his tongue, tracing along his human's lower lip. His *stella guida*'s slightly salty, masculine flavor burst across his taste buds, drawing a groan from him.

Mordecai lifted his head just a little to whisper, "Delicious."

Capturing Jeffrey's lips again, Mordecai felt a rush of satisfaction when his human parted for him. He eased his tongue into the man's mouth, flicking and darting about experimentally. Mordecai shuddered as the succulent flavor of his *stella guida* hit him fully, and his erection throbbed in time with the laps Jeffrey made against his tongue.

Needing more, needing pressure, Mordecai moved his right hand. He wrapped that arm around Jeffrey and, for the first time, took a liberty he'd never dreamed of. Mordecai palmed Jeffrey's butt cheek and pulled him closer, lifting him in the process.

Jeffrey fed Mordecai a moan. Lifting one leg, he wrapped it around Mordecai's waist. His arms twined over Mordecai's shoulders, and he rested his weight against him. The move opened Jeffrey's hips wide, allowing their bodies to slot together.

For the first time in his life, Mordecai felt another hard dick pressing insistently against his own, separated by so very little. With a thought, that cloth was gone. Mordecai removed everything from them both, and heat sizzled along his flesh everywhere Jeffrey touched against him.

Groaning, Jeffrey lifted his second leg and rocked his hips, rutting against him.

Mordecai's lust exploded as he recognized the trust Jeffrey was offering him. Clutching his human close, he widened his stance and planted his feet for balance. He rolled his hips, meeting Jeffrey's insistent thrusts.

Zings of heat cascaded along the length of his shaft. His groin goose bumped as his balls tingled. He felt an unfamiliar ache, and his head began to swim.

With a growl, Mordecai tore his mouth from Jeffrey's. He tipped his head back and groaned as his body flashed hot, his first orgasm crashing over him like a rogue wave. His legs trembled, and he had just enough wherewithal to turn and drop to the mattress.

Panting harshly, Mordecai shuddered and trembled. His erection beat in time with his heart, jerking as it spurted his seed between them. He moaned Jeffrey's name as bliss blanketed his psyche in ecstasy.

Mordecai slowly came back to himself, feeling a soft, gentle petting to his right wing. Peeling open eyelids he didn't remember closing, he peered up at Jeffrey. His human smiled at him, smugness in his expression.

Smiling back, Mordecai tried to get his brain back online. "No wonder Murdoch dragged Malakai away," he mumbled. "That was amazing."

"That *was* amazing," Jeffrey agreed, gliding his left palm down his wing. Mordecai noticed his right hand was behind his back as his human claimed, "And I'm pretty sure that was just the beginning."

Mordecai wasn't certain his senses could handle more, even though he knew what needed to happen to finish their bond. "What are you doing?" he asked curiously, noticing Jeffrey's arm moving a little. Then Mordecai felt the hard shaft riding his groin, and embarrassment filled him. "Oh, *stella guida*. I'm so sorry I did not please you."

"You pleased me, Mordecai," Jeffrey assured, cupping

Mordecai's jaw with his left hand. "Trust me. You did." With a wry smile, Jeffrey told him, "Some of that spunk you feel between us is mine."

Relief flooded Mordecai, and he sighed even as he smiled. Still, he couldn't help but point out, "But you're still hard."

"So are you." Jeffrey winked. "And I forgive you for removing our clothes because I sure wouldn't have wanted to come in my pants."

Mordecai grimaced, recalling Jeffrey's words about wanting to undress him. "I can clean us and reclothe us if you wish."

Jeffrey barked a laugh even as he shook his head. "That would be damn uncomfortable with my fingers in my ass."

Widening his eyes, surprise filling him, Mordecai lifted his head. "Really?"

Mordecai peered down the line of Jeffrey's naked backside and froze. His erection, just as hard as his *stella guida* had pointed out, twitched against his human's shaft. He found the stimulation painful in a pleasant way he never would have expected.

At some point during his orgasm, Mordecai must have moved his hands to Jeffrey's hips, but he couldn't resist sliding his right hand up and down the curve of his human's spine. He lifted his head a bit higher and stared at where his *stella guida* did indeed have two fingers in his chute. Sliding his hand to where Jeffrey penetrated himself, Mordecai teased his fingertips around his stretched ring.

Feeling the soft skin, hearing Jeffrey's hum of pleasure, Mordecai felt his shaft begin to ache once more.

"Jeffrey." Mordecai whispered his name like a benediction. "Oh, by the creator. That is . . ."

Mordecai's voice trailed off as he had no words to describe the delectable view. His *stella guida* prepared himself for his taking. Wanting to share in the experience, Mordecai murmured a few words, transporting slick from the tube of lube in the drawer and onto his palm.

When Mordecai dripped the liquid onto Jeffrey's fingers and hole, his lover hissed and froze. He met his human's gaze, who stared at him questioningly. Mordecai couldn't help it. He winked.

"There's lube in the nightstand," Mordecai revealed with a grin. "Malakai gave it to me. I used a spell to translocate it to my hand."

"Well, damn," Jeffrey whispered with wide eyes. "That's a nifty trick."

Mordecai pecked a kiss to Jeffrey's lips. "May I ease a finger into you, my *stella guida*?" His gut clenched just at the idea of feeling his human's heat wrapped around his finger. *And soon, my dick.* "I wish to feel you." After a second of hesitation, Mordecai added, "To learn how to stretch you and please you."

Jeffrey nibbled his bottom lip even as he nodded. "Okay." Then he removed his own fingers.

Pressing a finger into his human, Mordecai groaned as exquisite heat wrapped around his digit. His erection throbbed with anticipation. He eased a second finger in beside the first and began moving them in and out, and a shudder worked through him as he imagined that sensation on his shaft.

With a sigh, Jeffrey arched into his touch. He rested his clenched hands on either side of Mordecai's head. Pressing his forehead to Mordecai's collarbone, Jeffrey groaned and shuddered.

"Right there," Jeffrey gasped around another moan. "Yeah, that's the spot."

Mordecai realized he'd been massaging over a soft spongy area within Jeffrey's chute. *Ah, found his prostate.* Grinning with pride, Mordecai reveled in the knowledge that he was pleasing his *stella guida*.

Working that nub in earnest, Mordecai obeyed when Jeffrey urged him to work in a third finger. He gritted his teeth when the squeeze intensified. Desperation like he'd never felt before began to churn in his gut.

"Now," Jeffrey cried, shuddering above him. "Please, now. Or I'm going to come again."

More than willing to obey Jeffrey's urgings, Mordecai slipped his fingers from his human's body. He did his best to ignore the man's groan of obvious dismay. Grabbing his lover's hips, Mordecai rolled them and scooted them up the bed in one swift move.

Mordecai settled between Jeffrey's legs, who spread his thighs wide to accommodate him. As he grabbed his length and applied slick to it, he took in his *stella guida*'s heavy-lidded expression and the fine sheen of sweat covering his muscular body. He couldn't remember ever seeing anything more gorgeous than his flushed and needy human.

"Mine," Mordecai whispered huskily as he guided himself to Jeffrey's prepared hole. "All mine."

When his dick's swollen crown bumped his human's opening, Mordecai hissed at the stimulation. Staring between them, he murmured Jeffrey's name as he thrust. His *stella guida*'s body opened to him, and his flared head was swallowed in the tightest, sweetest grip he'd ever experienced.

Unable to help himself, Mordecai kept pushing, sinking deeper and deeper. When his smooth groin settled flush to Jeffrey's crack, he froze. His body shook with the effort to stay still, every instinct screaming at him to pull out and thrust back in again.

Jeffrey touched Mordecai's chin, and he met his human's gaze. With the sweetest, hungriest smile curving his lips, Jeffrey ordered, "Move."

Mordecai barked a harsh cry as he obeyed. Within a few thrusts, he lost any hope at finesse. He slid one arm under Jeffrey's hips, spread his wings for balance, and pounded into his *stella guida*.

His human's cries of delight echoed through the room, and Mordecai reveled in pleasing him as he lost all control.

CHAPTER TEN

Feeling a finger teasing at his asshole drew Jeffrey out of a really great dream of being sucked by a sexy man. He groaned softly and pushed back into the touch. To his pleasure, when he rocked forward again, a hot slick palm squeezed his dick.

Oh, this is so much better than any dream.

A low, husky chuckle sounded from behind Jeffrey.

Turning his head, Jeffrey smiled at the handsome angel waking him up in the best way possible. His chute muscles were stretched to a pleasant sting, telling him that Mordecai already had three fingers in him. His balls were already threatening to pull tight, responding to a combination of the squeezing tug on his shaft as well as the stimulation to his prostate.

And let's not forget the suckling on his claiming scar. Holy shit!

After getting off twice—once from frotting and once from fucking—Jeffrey hadn't expected to come a third time, no matter what Mordecai had told him about the claiming bite. He'd been wrong. He'd ended up damn near comatose for a good ten minutes.

They'd cuddled and talked, Mordecai sharing more about the nature of an angel as well as their duties. When Jeffrey had begun exploring his angel's gorgeous wings, he'd unwittingly started another round. Evidently, Mordecai loved the feel of Jeffrey petting his wings.

"Mord," Jeffrey muttered on a groan as Mordecai suckled

his claiming scar, dipping his thumbnail into his slit. "Pleeeease."

"Mmmm." Mordecai growled behind him. "I love reducing you to single words."

Before Jeffrey could beg Mordecai to hurry up, his lover was there, pushing into him. He sank into him in one long slow glide, teasing over his pleasure nub. At the same time, Mordecai reached around and cradled his ball sack.

During the course of their explorations the evening before, Mordecai had discovered how much Jeffrey loved for his nuts to be touched. He rolled his sack in his palm. He pinched the loose skin. Mordecai even gripped his balls in one of his large hands and tugged every-so-lightly.

Jeffrey groaned and arched, pushing into that bliss-inducing touch. His balls threatened to tighten, but due to Mordecai's grip, they couldn't. Heat pooled in Jeffrey's gut, and his dick throbbed.

A second later, Mordecai began reaming his ass, pegging his gland with each rut. His angel growled in his ear, slamming into him over and over. The man's huge rod stretched Jeffrey to capacity, sending his senses spiraling.

"*Stella guida,*" Mordecai hissed into his ear as he sank deep one last time.

Just as Jeffrey felt Mordecai's erection pulse within him, coating his rectum with burst after burst of hot seed, his angel released his balls. He moved his hand upward and gripped a nipple. While squeezing it, he nipped the claiming scar.

Shouting Mordecai's name, Jeffrey roared as his release surged through him. He clenched onto the member pulsing in his ass as his senses soared. Shudders racked him, and if it weren't for the strong arms holding him, he feared he would have flown away.

"Aww, Jeffrey," Mordecai purred into his ear. "You're

perfect, my *stella guida*. So perfect."

Before Jeffrey could catch his breath and respond—what the hell he would say, he didn't know—he felt Mordecai's canines sink into his flesh. The flash of pain instantly morphed into something else, something electric. His nipples beaded, his cock throbbed, and his balls tightened again.

Jeffrey felt his eyes roll to the back of his head as his second orgasm of the morning crashed over him.

Letting out a low moan, Jeffrey slowly swam back to wakefulness. He felt Mordecai nuzzling the back of his neck with his lips. His lover petted his stomach with one hand while playing along the grooves of his groin with the other.

"Back with me?" Mordecai rumbled in his ear.

"Yeah." Jeffrey let out a low sigh. "How long was I out?"

Mordecai hummed. "Not long. A few minutes," he revealed. "I love driving you out of your mind with bliss."

Jeffrey heard the smug satisfaction in Mordecai's tone. Smiling and humming, he just bet the angel did. His lover was a quick study and an eager pupil, learning about Jeffrey's body with astonishing speed.

Turning his head, Jeffrey tilted his head up and met Mordecai's gaze. "Good morning."

Mordecai tilted his head up and pressed a kiss to Jeffrey's lips, obviously picking up on what he wanted. "Good morning, my *stella guida*." Gently, Mordecai eased his prick from Jeffrey's body, then encouraged him to roll until he was draped over Mordecai's wide torso, their legs tangling intimately. As the angel threaded his fingers through Jeffrey's hair, he asked, "What are your plans for today? Would you like to explore the ranch activities?"

It was on the tip of Jeffrey's tongue to say yes. Then he recalled what day it was. "Shit. What time is it?" He popped his head up, looking toward the nightstand. Seeing the time,

Jeffrey groaned and pushed to a sitting position. "Damn it. I'm going to be late for work."

There was no way Jeffrey would be able to make the drive home, get cleaned up, and make it to the job site. With a grimace, he started shuffling to the side of the bed. "I'm sorry, Mordecai," Jeffrey stated, disappointment filling him that their interlude had to end. "I gotta go." As he stood, he turned and faced Mordecai, who was rising nearby. "Can I borrow the SUV? I promise I'll bring it back tonight." Realizing how presumptuous that sounded, Jeffrey quickly added, "Uh, if you don't mind me returning tonight."

Mordecai rounded the bed with narrowed eyes. "You are my *stella guida,*" he growled. "Of course, I want you by my side." Then he wrapped his arms around Jeffrey, as well as his wings. "But taking the SUV won't be necessary."

"But— " Jeffrey began, but Mordecai interrupted him.

"Allow me to introduce you to lei line travel."

In the next instant, the world around Jeffrey faded. He blinked, his mind going swimmy. If Mordecai's arms hadn't been firmly around him, Jeffrey feared he would have collapsed.

As it was, when the world appeared around Jeffrey once more, he was immediately swung into Mordecai's arms. He stared in shock as he watched the angel stride through his back yard and onto his porch. With a touch to the door, Mordecai had it open, even though Jeffrey was very certain he'd left it locked.

"How . . . how'd you do that?" Jeffrey whispered in shock. Mordecai didn't stop as he carried him through his mud room, dining room, and along a hallway, obviously knowing exactly where to go. "Mordecai?"

"Sorry to startle you, Jeffrey." Mordecai smiled down at him as he walked into Jeffrey's attached ensuite. "But this way, you don't have to worry about returning the coven's

SUV, and I can have dinner waiting for you after you return." Setting Jeffrey onto his feet, Mordecai asked, as if what had happened was the most natural thing in the world, "Do you work this weekend? We could go fishing or horseback riding at the ranch. Would you like me to sign us up for their chuckwagon dinner excursion on any particular evening?"

"Uh, can you explain the whole lei line thing again?" Jeffrey had no idea what that meant. Glancing between their nude bodies, he frowned as he reached in and turned on the water. "And why were we walking outside naked? Someone could have seen us." As Jeffrey stepped under the shower, he grumbled, "And no one should see you naked except me."

Mordecai hummed, the sound one of clear pleasure. "I find I'm extremely pleased to hear and scent your jealousy. Have no fear, my *stella guida.* I placed us under a glamour. No one could see us unless they used magick." Leaning against the bathroom wall, he stared openly as Jeffrey grabbed the washcloth and soap and began scrubbing himself down. "And I'd join you, but then you'd never get to work on time."

"Magick, huh?" Jeffrey wanted to ask about that, but he wasn't certain he had time for the answer. Instead, he decided to go with, "What are people who use magick called?"

"Witches and warlocks," Mordecai told him.

Of course.

"And these lei line things?"

Mordecai began explaining how lines of power crisscrossed the globe. Those with powerful magickal abilities could use them to transport themselves, and sometimes others, from one place to another nearly instantly. For the most part, they were only utilized by angels and demons.

Right. Those again.

Jeffrey figured that made sense. If there were angels, there had to be demons. Then he recalled how demons weren't inherently evil, but the minions of the Four Horsemen of the Apocalypse.

Geez, there's so much to remember.

"Uh, so, yeah," Jeffrey replied, recalling some of Mordecai's questions. "If we can get in on that chuckwagon dinner thing tonight, that'd be really cool." He remembered reading about the hay wagon and open-air meal cooked over a fire on the ranch's website the prior year when he'd looked into staying there. It had sounded fun. Grinning wryly at Mordecai, Jeffrey added, "And I'm supposed to be meeting with Charles after work at the gym, but I can cancel if you want me to. I worked out last night and this morning enough to make up for it."

Mordecai smirked as he ran his gaze hungrily over Jeffrey's wet body. "It was a lot of fun, too." Then he cocked his head and asked, "Why don't you ask Charles to join us for dinner at the ranch?" Rubbing the back of his neck, Mordecai admitted, "Charles is the one I'm tasked to stay close to while he figures out something in his life. I thought it was his sexuality, but now I'm not so sure."

"Huh. I think Charles is comfortable in that area," Jeffrey told Mordecai, thinking of their conversations. "And I'll ask him." He recalled Mordecai telling him that an angel could be tasked by the creator to help a specific person, and for Mordecai, it was Charles who'd brought him to the region. Jeffrey would be happy to help out his angel. "I'm sure spending time with him is crucial to figuring out the best way to help him."

"Thank you for understanding, Jeffrey."

With a smile and nod, Jeffrey turned off the water, grabbed a towel, and began drying himself. A second later, he was dry and dressed, and Mordecai was giving him a roguish smile.

Recalling how Mordecai had cleaned them of cum and

lube the evening before with just a quick thought, Jeffrey asked, "How come you didn't just clean me up, too?"

Mordecai growled as he pinned Jeffrey with a hungry look. "And miss seeing you naked and wet in the shower?"

Jeffrey laughed, conceding the point.

Hours later, Jeffrey wrapped up his phone call with Charles. His buddy had agreed to join them at the ranch as opposed to working out that evening. Just as he was about to say goodbye, Jeffrey saw a *BMW* that he recognized pull up in front of his job site.

As the driver exited, Jeffrey muttered into the phone, "Why the hell would Reagan be at my job site?"

"Reagan? Reagan Suthers?" Charles asked, obviously for clarification.

"Yup." Seeing the angry, calculating glint in Reagan's brown eyes as he sauntered toward Jeffrey, an uncomfortable twist formed in Jeffrey's gut. Having always listened to his instincts before, he murmured, "I'm gonna put you on speaker. Hang on a sec, would ya?"

"Sure, man."

Then Jeffrey placed the call on speaker and settled it in his shirt pocket. "Hey, Reagan," Jeffrey greeted warily. "You're a little out of place here."

The man was, too. He wore a nice suit and tie. His high-end dress shoes definitely weren't designed for the dirt and mud of a landscaping job.

"Hello, Jeffrey," Reagan replied, his smile appearing creepy. "I told you not to try to get close to Mordecai. The angel is mine."

Jeffrey gasped, shocked that not only did Reagan know what Mordecai was but that he somehow knew that they'd been together.

In the same instant, Reagan lifted his hand from his pocket. He cupped it in the air between their heads and blew. A puff of blue dust flew into the air.

As Jeffrey choked on the strange powder, anger coursed through him. He prayed whatever shit that was wouldn't compromise his ability to do his job.

"What the fuck?" Jeffrey snarled.

"Shut up," Reagan snarled.

Jeffrey felt his jaw snap shut, and no matter how hard he tried, he couldn't open it again.

"Follow me and get in the passenger side of my car," Reagan stated next.

Jeffrey's mind reeled as his body started obeying the order. His legs moved of their own accord, and he found himself walking toward the vehicle.

Fortunately, Jeffrey realized his hands and arms were still his own. He yanked his phone from his pocket and quickly began typing a message to Charles, since his number was still on the display.

Contact Mordecai. Tell him Reagan kid –

"Give me that," Reagan demanded, holding out his hand.

Jeffrey retained just enough self-control to hit the send button before he handed the phone to Reagan.

Just what the hell is going on?

Chapter Eleven

Hearing his phone trill from his pocket, Mordecai immediately thought of Jeffrey and smiled. He didn't know of anyone else who would call him in the middle of the day. Pulling out his phone, he lifted a finger, silently asking Malakai to hang on a second.

Mordecai read the display, and the smile slipped from his features. While he'd given Charles his phone number, he couldn't imagine why the human would be calling him. He thought he would need to spend at least two more occasions with him before Charles would feel comfortable contacting him.

With the hairs on his nape suddenly standing on end, Mordecai took the call. "Hello, Charles," he greeted. Then a thought occurred to him. "Are you calling to confirm on joining us for the chuckwagon dinner tonight?"

Mordecai had already made certain his last-minute request could be accommodated by the vampires. Normally, there was a sign-up sheet hung the day before. It filled fast, and it was first come, first served.

Fortunately, a subtle mental push by one of the vampires had convinced a family of three to wait until the following day.

"No, uh, yeah." The normally eloquent man—he was an attorney, after all—stumbled with his words, making Mordecai frown. Charles blew out a harsh breath, easily heard through the line, then tried again. "Yes, I talked to Jeffrey, and he asked about rescheduling our workout and going on that chuckwagon dinner thing, and it sounds like fun." Charles scoffed as he admitted, "I always put off cardio, even though it's the most important."

Considering Mordecai had never needed to work out like that—sure, he'd worked to hone his ability with a sword, but that was different—he didn't know anything about cardio. "Okay." He hesitated a second before adding, "I'm glad to hear you can make it."

"Yeah, thanks, but that's not why I'm calling," Charles revealed. "It's Jeffrey."

Mordecai's gut twisted uncomfortably, and his heartrate sped up. "What about Jeffrey?"

"Reagan showed up at his job site during Jeffrey's lunch break, while I was talking to him on the phone." Charles sounded a mixture of confused and worried. "Somehow, Reagan must have known you and Jeffrey went on a date last night because he said Jeffrey shouldn't have tried to get close to you. Then he said this weird shit about the angel being his." Before Mordecai could even guess how to explain that, Charles continued, "Then he started ordering Jeffrey around, and I got this weird text from Jeff to call you before the line disconnected." The more he talked, the more worry caused Charles's voice to tighten. "He told me to call you. To tell you he'd been kid. Now I think that means Reagan was trying to kidnap Jeffrey, but why would my buddy go with him?"

"Thank you for contacting me, Charles," Mordecai cut into the human's confused rambling. "I'll contact him. Whatever it is, I'll get it sorted."

"Yeah, okay." Charles hesitated a second before asking, "Should I call the cops?"

"No," Mordecai immediately ordered. If this Reagan guy knew about angels, there was no way he wanted the cops involved. When Mordecai heard Charles start to question him, he quickly assured, "We don't want to contact the cops if everything is fine, and it's just a miscommunication."

"You'll let me know what's going on, right?"

Upon hearing Charles's demand, Mordecai smiled. The human had a decent heart. He hoped he could figure out what the man's issue was and help him.

"Yes," Mordecai assured. "I'll let you know what's happening."

"Okay. Thanks, man."

After Charles disconnected the call, Mordecai met Malakai's gaze.

His fellow angel's frown told him that the other male had heard everything that Charles had said. Malakai must have used his telepathic connection to contact Murdoch, for the vampire appeared, rounding the corner of the cabin. Once Murdoch was close enough, Malakai wrapped his arm around him, then held up his hand, palm up.

Mordecai grabbed the other angel's hand. Closing his eyes, he sought out the link between himself and his *stella guida*. He found it instantly, although there was a strange quality to it. It almost felt . . . faded . . . or tainted in some way, as if someone was attempting to tamper with their connection.

A low growl rumbled from Mordecai's throat as he mentally latched onto a lei line. He felt Malakai's presence join him as he zipped toward Jeffrey's location. Mordecai had just enough presence of mind not to appear outright. Instead, he used a glamour to keep himself hidden as he surveyed the area.

What Mordecai saw caused a growl to roll through his chest.

A dark-haired human stood in the middle of a small clearing amidst a copse of trees. He stood over a shirtless Jeffrey who was sprawled on a stone table, and he was painting sigils on his *stella guida*'s chest. The man was copying the sigils onto his own bare chest. Each time he did it, the guy murmured a chant, and Mordecai felt an odd tug on his bond with Jeffrey.

Realization hit Mordecai, and he released his glamour. He also changed his clothing. His polo shirt disappeared to be replaced by a leather vest. His jeans turned into a skirt of leather pleats, and he barely resisted drawing the sword that appeared at his waist.

Stalking forward, Mordecai snapped, "You dare attempt to tamper with the bond gifted by the Fates?"

To his knowledge, there was nothing that would break the bond granted between soul mates. Still, even trying was taboo. The gift of finding your other half was sacrosanct. Even upon death, the pair would be resurrected close enough together to find each other again.

To Mordecai's surprise, the man turned and grinned at him. "There's nothing that can break the bond of a fated pair." His dark eyes swept over Mordecai's body, and a lecherous expression crossed his features. "But that doesn't mean I can't still use you."

Mordecai sneered at the stupid human, swiftly closing the gap between them.

Before Mordecai could grab the man, the human blew a cloud of blue dust into his face. Mordecai reared back and shook his head, coughing in surprise. The man laughed, his dark eyes gleaming manically.

"I am Reagan Suthers, and you, angel, will do exactly as I say." With a smug smirk curving his features, Reagan ordered, "Take off your clothes. I want to check out what's mine from now on."

For just an instant, Mordecai felt an odd desire to obey. His fingers twitched, and he lifted a hand toward his belt. Then he shook his head once, realizing what it was. After murmuring a counter-compulsion spell, Mordecai cleared his mind of the desire to obey.

"Your foul concoctions will not work on me, Reagan Suthers," Mordecai declared before lunging forward again.

Reagan was faster than he looked. Curling his lip, the warlock skittered around the table. A second later, he held a knife in his hand, and he pressed it to Jeffrey's throat.

While Jeffrey continued to lie motionless, the fear in his eyes tore at something deep within Mordecai. He froze, waiting, shuffling through spells within his mind.

"Obey me, angel," Reagan ordered. His brown eyes narrowed menacingly. "Or I will slit Jeffrey's throat, and you will have to live eternity with the knowledge that you failed your *stella guida.*"

"You know only pieces about our kind if you think that will stop me from destroying you, Reagan." Mordecai took a menacing step forward. "The fact that Jeffrey still breathes is the only thing that is keeping you alive."

"Don't test me, angel," Reagan declared. A second later, a thin dribble of blood trickled down the side of Jeffrey's neck. "You won't like the consequences."

Mordecai froze, and Reagan's lips curved into a cruel smile. His eyes gleamed with satisfaction. Mordecai knew the human had thought he'd won.

Except, he hadn't.

After all, Mordecai wasn't alone. All he'd needed to do was distract the human. By keeping him focused on Mordecai, the warlock wouldn't notice the signatures of two other paranormals.

A second later, Malakai appeared behind Reagan. He grabbed him from behind as Murdoch swooped in and stabbed his knife-like talons through the warlock's forearm. As Malakai pulled a screaming Reagan backward, Murdoch used the way he'd skewered the man to force his arm up and the knife away from Jeffrey's throat.

Mordecai took the opening. Lunging forward, he swept Jeffrey into his arms and off the stone platform. He cradled his *stella guida* close as he rushed away from the pair subduing the warlock.

Pausing at the edge of the meadow, Mordecai uttered his cleaning spell. Instantly, Jeffrey's flesh gleamed, cleared of the hated sigils. His next words were a spell to remove the compulsion he figured Jeffrey had to be under.

Jeffrey gasped a breath. His eyes widened, and he flung his arms around Mordecai's neck. He clung as he trembled in his hold.

"Wh-What the h-hell just happened?" Jeffrey managed to stutter. Peering up at Mordecai, he admitted, "I-I couldn't do anything but what Reagan told me to do. I—" Jeffrey stopped and shook his head, fear rolling off of him in waves.

"You're safe now, Jeffrey. I promise," Mordecai assured, rubbing his palm over his human's side soothingly. "I have you. I'm sorry that happened to you." Even with him safe in his arms, Mordecai couldn't stop touching him. "You're safe."

After a moment, Jeffrey's trembling stopped, although his grip didn't loosen. He held Mordecai's gaze. "He blew dust into my face, and then . . . it was like my body wasn't my own." Frowning, Jeffrey asked, "How is that possible?"

"Reagan is a warlock," Mordecai explained softly. A glance over his shoulder showed him a bound, gagged, and unconscious Reagan slung over Murdoch's shoulder. Malakai offered him a small smile and nod. "Thank you, my brother."

"You're welcome, Mordecai." Malakai took a few steps closer, then stopped. The other angel probably understood how territorial Mordecai was feeling. "I'm honored to assist." Then Malakai glanced back at Murdoch. "We both are, and don't worry about Reagan. We'll take him to Master Jaymes. Reagan will be dealt with in accordance to his crimes."

Mordecai knew what that meant. For attempting to come between fated mates, there was only one punishment.

Death.

"Thank you," Mordecai repeated.

Malakai nodded again before returning to Murdoch. With his arm slung around his vampire's shoulders, they disappeared.

Mordecai returned his focus to Jeffrey. "Reagan used an enchanted dust to compel you to obey. I've cleared it from your system." After a second of hesitation, he added, "As our bond strengthens, you'll be able to repel such spells. I'll teach you."

Jeffrey sagged against him, cuddling into his chest. "Good. Because I never want to be vulnerable like that again."

Silently, Mordecai agreed.

With another thought, Mordecai returned them to the cabin at the ranch. He didn't stop until they were both in the shower. While he'd technically cleared Jeffrey's body of sweat and debris, Mordecai needed to check over his *stella guida* the old-fashioned way—with his hands, lips, tongue, and teeth.

Chapter Twelve

Jeffrey sat on the cabin's small front porch, drinking a beer. With his foot on the railing in front of him, he flexed and relaxed his thigh muscle. He kept the swinging bench moving in a slow, calming rhythm.

As Jeffrey panned his attention over the ranch yard, he could see the appeal. There were a dozen cabins scattered around the couple of acres. The one Mordecai occupied happened to be the furthest out, giving them an extra modicum of privacy. There were half a dozen barns, a couple for ranch horses and those in training, a couple for trail horses, one for breeding, and one for foaling.

There were plenty of happy people milling about, talking amongst themselves, or heading to their next activity.

Watching them, Jeffrey realized that most of them probably had no idea that they were surrounded by vampires. He smiled, amazed at the coven's operation. The group had a steady source of blood donors nearly all year round in the way of single, friendly, and often-times flirty guests.

God, how crazy it is to be in the know.

Smiling to himself, Jeffrey took another swig of beer. He was waiting for Mordecai to return from his meeting with Master Jaymes. Jeffrey had been introduced to the vampire master and his human beloved, Paul, after Mordecai had finished examining him from head to toe in the shower.

Jeffrey shifted in his chair, feeling the stretch in his ass. His angel had hammered his hole, betraying how he'd feared for him. That warmed him more than Jeffrey could possibly explain.

My angel needs me, just as I'm coming to need him.

"How are you holding up?" Mordecai asked, revealing his presence.

Smiling up at Mordecai, Jeffrey patted the bench seat beside him. Mordecai immediately sat, and Jeffrey leaned against his side, reveling in the feel of his angel's arm around him.

"I'm much better now," Jeffrey replied softly. "What happened with Reagan?"

Jeffrey knew he would be judged in the paranormal way, because not only was he a magick user, but he also knew of the paranormal world. As it turned out, not all witches and warlocks knew about other things that went bump in the night.

"Reagan will be put to death for his crimes," Mordecai answered softly, rubbing his hand over Jeffrey's opposite shoulder soothingly. "There's no recourse for someone who attempted to manipulate our bond in such a way."

Nodding, Jeffrey brought his beer to his lips. After taking a swig of beer, he offered it to Mordecai. His angel took the bottle and sipped it. He grunted and handed it back.

"I prefer honeyed mead," Mordecai admitted. "But some of the red wines they have in this realm aren't too bad."

Jeffrey smiled, chuckling softly. He opened his mouth, then spotted the sedan rolling toward them. He recognized it as Charles's.

"Remember, according to the way the vampires altered the memories of those at the job site, Reagan attacked you with a garden rake." Mordecai reminded him of the tale the vampires weaved so no one would question why Jeffrey hadn't returned to work that afternoon. "You dodged, but it still hit you across your shoulders. You went to the hospital to get checked out."

Smirking, Jeffrey held up his beer. "Should I be drinking

alcohol?"

"You refused pain meds," Mordecai replied easily.

Jeffrey scoffed. "For an angel, you lie well." Watching Charles exit the vehicle, he kept his voice low.

Mordecai winced. "I'm not the one who told the lie," he murmured, also keeping his voice low. "For the sake of anonymity, I'm just not correcting it."

Wincing, Jeffrey focused on Mordecai. "I'm sorry. I meant to tease." He touched his lover's jaw. "I didn't mean to offend."

"I know." Mordecai leaned down and pressed a chaste kiss to Jeffrey's lips. When he straightened, he was smiling, "We are still learning about each other."

Returning his angel's smile, Jeffrey nodded. "That we are." Then he turned his attention to Charles, who'd paused halfway between his car and the steps. "Hey, Charles." Jeffrey rose and held up his nearly empty bottle. "Want a beer for the hay ride?"

Jeffrey had heard it was allowed if the guests gained permission ahead of time and weren't openly intoxicated. After all, the activity was a family affair.

Charles nodded, closing the distance and pausing at the bottom of the steps. "That'd be great, Jeff." Shoving his hands into his pockets, he asked, "What the hell happened with Reagan?"

"I'll get the beers," Mordecai offered, heading into the house.

Considering the way Mordecai left the front door open, Jeffrey knew his angel would be able to hear every word he said. He also guessed that the man would corroborate whatever version of events Jeffrey passed on to his friend. He decided to keep it simple and relatively vague.

"Thanks for calling Mordecai for me," Jeffrey went with. "His support meant a lot to me." Scoffing, he shook his head as he frowned. "Reagan totally went off the jealousy deep end. He threatened me to try to get me to walk away from Mordecai." After rolling his eyes, Jeffrey finished his beer.

With impeccable timing, Mordecai appeared before Charles could ask more questions. "Here's your beer, Charles." He leaned against the porch rail and held it out. "You ready for supper?"

As if on cue, Jeffrey's stomach rumbled. "*I* am." He leaned in the doorway and set the empty on the side table by the door. Then he closed the door, making certain to lock it. "Thanks."

Taking the already-opened bottle from Mordecai, Jeffrey noticed the angel had a single-serving bottle of merlot in hand.

Guess the angel couldn't find any honeyed mead.

"I'm definitely ready," Charles answered as he lowered the bottle from his lips. "Marylou was supposed to order lunch for our noon meeting, but she thought it was being handled by Gayle." Shaking his head, Charles grumbled, "By the time the food arrived, I had to head to a video conference call. When I got done, the food was gone, so I had to settle for a granola bar from the vending machine. I'm starved."

"Well, these guys serve plenty of food," Mordecai told him, easing his arm around Jeffrey's waist. "And I hear this chuckwagon dinner is plenty good."

With a laugh, Charles revealed, "I haven't done anything like this since I was a kid." He fell into step with them as they moved toward the staging area. "Hey, Jeff." Charles bumped his elbow into him lightly. "I'm glad you're okay."

"Thanks, man." Jeffrey smiled at his buddy. "Me, too."

"You charging Reagan?"

"Hell, yeah, man." Jeffrey growled under his breath. "Not gonna let that rat bastard get away with shit." Thankfully, they were closing in on the area which was filled with families, so Jeffrey changed the subject. "Mordecai mentioned you're not a fan of cardio. How are you going to run a marathon with me if you don't keep up on your cardio?"

Charles blanched, his eyes widening. "A marathon?" Then he must have realized Jeffrey was teasing, for he rolled his eyes and shook his head. "Ha, ha, ha."

Jeffrey grinned.

Sitting on a hay bale between Mordecai and Charles, Jeffrey watched as a black-haired woman settled on his buddy's other side just before the wagon lurched forward, making him appreciate Mordecai's arm around his shoulders. He knew he'd seen her around the ranch, but he couldn't place her. Mordecai seemed to have no such trouble.

"Are you on chaperone duty tonight, Clarice?"

Clarice smiled brightly. "I am. Good thing, too." Her rich, chocolate-brown-eyed gaze landed on Charles. She nudged her shoulder against Charles's. "And who are you, handsome beloved?"

"Uh." For a second, Charles stared at Clarice, seemingly tongue-tied. "Ch-Charles." He cleared his throat and managed a warm smile. "Charles Rickter." He held out his hand. "You work here, Clarice?"

Taking Charles's hand, Clarice nodded. "I do. No better place to be than out here in the country," she told him. "Fresh air. Nature. And I *love* meeting new people."

Jeffrey definitely heard the innuendo in her voice. Then her words registered. Squeezing Mordecai's thigh, he gained his angel's attention. He arched one brow and discreetly mouthed, *beloved*?

Mordecai smiled warmly and nodded once. Evidently, his lover had noticed the comment as well.

For some reason, Jeffrey appreciated that. He found he enjoyed Charles's company, and being able to discuss paranormal things with him would be even better. Turning his attention back to the pair, Jeffrey noticed they were chatting easily, flirting lightly with each other.

When there was a lull in the conversation, Jeffrey couldn't help but ask, "So, what do people do around the campfire, Clarice?" He smiled at her when her attention landed on him. "Tell ghost stories?"

"Well, it's happened on occasion," Clarice replied slowly, a small smile curving her full lips. She tucked a strand of black hair behind her ear that had escaped her low-hanging ponytail. "Or stories about other things that go bump in the night." With a wink, Clarice focused on Charles. "Got any favorites, Charles? Like vampires or werewolves or something?"

To Jeffrey's surprise, Charles grimaced and quickly shook his head. "Definitely no on the vampires." Evidently, his buddy noticed their surprised looks, for he quickly added, "The other two are fine, but no vampires, please." Charles shuddered dramatically. "Just the idea of blood makes me—" He paused and grimaced. Focusing on Jeffrey, Charles asked, "Remember that time you scraped your knuckles on the weight machine?" His eyes going wide, Charles admitted, "It took everything in me not to hurl when I saw you wiping it on your sweat towel."

Jeffrey gaped even as he nodded slowly. "Yeah," he murmured, recalling the incident. "I do seem to recall you going really pale."

Charles nodded, while smiling sheepishly at Clarice. "Sorry. Blood is just really not my thing."

"Oh," Clarice replied softly. She smiled gamely, trying to hide her concern. "Well, um." After clearing her throat, Clarice continued, "There are plenty of other types of stories."

"Yeah, totally." Charles grinned, completely oblivious.

"Can't wait."

Clarice glanced between him and Mordecai questioningly before returning her focus to Charles.

Jeffrey peered up at Mordecai, noticing his speculative expression. His angel peered intently at Charles, and his eyes narrowed just a smidge. Jeffrey just bet that his angel had picked up on some thought from his buddy. He suddenly really wished he knew what Charles might have been thinking.

Afraid of blood and the beloved of a vampire.

Well, well, well. It seems that's what Mordecai will need to help Charles with. The acceptance of the paranormal, vampires in particular, and his fear of blood.

As Mordecai glanced Jeffrey's way, arching a brow in silent question, Jeffrey smiled. He squeezed his angel's thigh and nudged him with his shoulder encouragingly.

Yup. I'll be with you to help every step of the way.

Mordecai beamed, having clearly heard him.

Jeffrey grinned back.

About the Author

Charlie started writing fantasy when she was eight, and after stumbling onto her first erotic romance at age nineteen, she realized her true calling. She now focuses on writing gay erotic romance, normally of the paranormal variety, with heroes of all kinds. With the help and support of her husband, Charlie finally fulfilled one of her life-long goals . . . move to acreage with her horses. You can often find her curled up with her laptop and a cup of tea or glass of wine, creating her next adventure. Charlie enjoys exploring the mountains of her new Oregon home on horseback, 4-wheeler, or motorcycle.

She can be reached at ch.richards2010@yahoo.com

Or visit her at www.charlie-richards.com.

www.ingramcontent.com/pod-product-compliance
Lightning Source LLC
Chambersburg PA
CBHW070519130626
46555CB00003B/1288
* 9 7 8 1 4 8 7 4 3 7 9 5 4 *